kal
aaj aur
kal

CYRUS
BROACHA

RANDOM HOUSE INDIA

Published by Random House India in 2010
2468 10 9753

Random House Publishers India Private Limited
MindMill Corporate Tower, 2nd Floor, Plot No 24A
Sector 16A, Noida 201301, UP

Random House Group Limited
20 Vauxhall Bridge Road
London SW1V 2SA
United Kingdom

978 81 8400 0986

Typeset in Sabon by InoSoft Systems, Noida

Printed and bound in India by Replika Press

For my wonderful parents, Olivia and Farrokh,
my Shahenshah Mikhaail, my Princess Maya,
and also Ruffo and Ayesha.

And for Volpi, 'see you on the terrace soon'.

preface

The author has asked me to write a note on his behalf as he's not feeling well.

First and foremost, the author is no longer a woman.

Second, he wrote this book under severe duress. His wife had an ingrown toenail that caused her to scream the whole time he was writing, and often the author couldn't hear his own words.

Third, the book was intended as a murder mystery, but due to the author's revulsion towards blood, it was adapted into a historical documentary with elements of drama, melodrama, but none whatsoever of lovemaking.

Fourth, all the characters portrayed in this book are fictitious, including the real ones. Especially the real ones.

Fifth, the author traces the journey of a young boy from adolescence to manhood and beyond, until eventually the young boy realizes that adolescence is far more fun and returns to it.

Sixth, and this is very important so pay close attention—there is no 'sixth'...

Now in the words of the author's probable father, Elvis Presley, 'Read on.'

prologue

In many ways, Karl and Kunal were like most boys their age. They shared a passion for the four things schoolboys seem to love most: bunking class, films, food, and pornography. And growing up in 1980s India—when people went to the movies only to watch Amitabh Bachchan—they must have been among Amitabh's biggest fans. That Amitabh was the King of the silver screen was a plain fact, just as night followed day, and Marlon Brando once weighed less than 400 pounds.

The two boys were entranced by a film called *Amar Akbar Anthony* in which Amitabh played a heroic vagabond, Anthony. It was at about this time that Karl discovered his passion for theatre. The noblest of reasons drew him to the stage: the need to perform and express himself but chiefly, the desire to bunk class. It was well known that anyone who was chosen for the school play would get to bunk the last two periods of the day, which were used for rehearsal.

The play that year was *The Frog Prince* and the parts up for audition were for the princess, the prince, and the frog. The princess's role suited Karl's artistic temperament the best, as it involved lying supine with eyes closed for the better part of the play, and only occasionally pushing away the frog in disgust. However, the school didn't want to waste money on a wig, so a real female was used. The next role that beckoned was the prince's. It was one of those forceful quality-over-quantity roles. You appeared on stage for a total of seven seconds, and that too at the fag end of the play. No great thespian skill seemed necessary: the entire act consisted of opening one's eyes and hugging the princess, after glimpsing whom one felt tempted, in any case, to shut one's eyes immediately.

But the drama teacher, Mrs Sahyani, took one look at Karl and shrieked ecstatically, 'There's my frog!' This was followed almost immediately by, 'Stop my frog!' as Karl prepared to flee, and, finally, 'Somebody catch my frog, pin him down, and bring him here ASAP!'

Mrs Sahyani looked proprietorially down at her frog while it tried to explain, in vain, that it had never played a frog before. In fact, Karl had never really known a frog and didn't even know of anyone who might. Furthermore, he couldn't distinguish between a male frog and a female frog, or between a frog and a toad. He ranted on about his family being more of a dog family than a frog family, and said that if he had to play the part of an animal, he would be far more accomplished as a goldfish or an elephant. When all this fell on deaf but finely groomed ears, he offered Mrs Sahyani a 'compromise candidate'. A boy who, Karl assured Mrs Sahyani, would play the part perfectly—his best friend, supporter, and confidant,

Kunal. Mrs Sahyani would have none of that. She cast him with immediate effect.

Mrs Sahyani was a realist. And a frog would have to appear shorter than the other actors. Thus it came to pass that a dismayed Karl suddenly found himself in a half-squat position on an empty stage during the last hour of school.

After the play was performed, Karl, like most great actors, made a smooth transition into his next role—from a frog to Anthony. His friend Kunal had styled himself after the other leading heart-throb in *Amar Akbar Anthony*, Vinod Khanna, who played Amar. Karl started referring to himself both in the third person and as Anthony. He also began to make definitive and dramatic statements. If told that dinner was ready, he would reply, 'Dinner may be ready, but Anthony isn't.' His father Jehaan, an English movie buff, once asked in perplexity, 'But who is Anthony?' To which Karl responded with a flick of his fringe using a comb, 'This is Anthony.' An exasperated Jehaan asked, 'Your comb is called Anthony?' Karl drew very close to his father's face, grit his teeth, pulled out a tiny hand mirror, and peering into it, murmured, '*This* is Anthony.' The pater was confused. '*I* am Anthony?' Karl then performed a military-like about turn and strode away in what he imagined to be an 'Amitabh Bachchan stride'. The Anthony fixation didn't end there. Twice his mother was summoned to school as her errant son had signed his project as the work of 'Anthony Gonsalves', not Karl Marshall.

Kunal, for his part, at the age of twelve, already

weighed more than Vinod Khanna ever would, but that didn't stop him emulating 'Inspector Amar'. To play the part, Kunal would wear his mother's sunglasses, which were about the size of a table fan. Amar and Anthony, one with his face concealed by a woman's shades, and the other with his affected swagger, did well with the ladies though. The girls enjoyed calling the pair by their screen names. Other boys, of course, felt that dried fish may have been cooler.

The Beatles once wrote, 'What would you do if I sang out of tune, would you stand up and walk out on me?' As far as Karl was concerned, the answer was certainly a 'yes', particularly if the question was asked by his rather top-heavy best friend, Kunal. The two boys were inseparable. But while Karl was ordinary looking, boyish, and goofy, Kunal was rotund, with a large, round face, rounder torso, and grasshopper-thin legs. Ah, those legs! Perhaps jeans weren't necessary—a pair of socks may have fitted snugly enough. In fact, Karl often rather unkindly asked the other kids to look at Kunal from a distance, whence his two spindly legs looked like one. Kunal had inherited his shape from his father—except for the difference of an inch in height, they shared exactly the same figure.

But that's enough about Kunal. This isn't his story. He didn't commission me to write it, Karl did. So let's get this straight. This tale is all about Karl, the *Karl Katha*, the *Karl-nama*. It's Karl's story.

The only damn problem is that Kunal's a big part of it.

chapter 1

Jehaan and Karl shared a fairly close father–son relationship, although their roles depended on their moods and were often reversed.

Jehaan Marshall was a Senior Copywriter at a distinguished advertising agency called D'Souza's in Mumbai. As a young man, Jehaan had wanted to be an operatic tenor and had initially modelled himself on Mario Del Monaco. During his teenage years, his voice became both sweeter and more lyrical (or so he thought), and he switched to Giuseppe Di Stefano. Sadly, in 1950s' India, you couldn't find three people who could pronounce 'Giuseppe', and his passion didn't get much encouragement except from his neighbour Sarabjeet Kaur, who would make the young Jehaan belt out 'Di Quella Pira' just to enrage her husband. At family get-togethers, Jehaan was a great hit. He was treated like a sound system. 'Jehaan, sing "Santa Lucia".' 'Jehaan, sing "Ma'appari".' 'Give us "O Sole Mio".' And most often, 'For God's sake Jehaan, STOP singing.'

On his fifteenth birthday, Jehaan fell in love with his neighbour Priya. Normally, this may have been quite acceptable, except that Priya was 44 years old and a mother of three. Priya lived in the building opposite Jehaan's, and exactly one floor higher. Since the flats were diagonally across from each other, in order to get a glimpse of Priya, Jehaan would have to wriggle—much like an eel—into a compact accordion-like position, with his back on the window rail and his nose pointing up at the sky. Since getting into this position took him about 50 seconds, there would occasionally be a slip 'twixt the cup and the lip. In an upright position, he'd vaguely see Priya, but by the time he had contorted his body, Priya might have been replaced by her husband, Mr Godhwani, whom the neighbourhood commonly referred to as The Hairy Beast. Nothing could kill a fifteen-year-old's fantasy faster than the sight of Mr Godhwani's torso. Of course, no one had ever seen Mr Godhwani's torso, least of all Mr Godhwani himself, because it was completely buried in a forest of hair. It was said (and only half in jest) that at funerals, he wouldn't have to wear a black shirt. A black pair of trousers and nothing on top would suffice. One lucky day, from his contortionist's position, Jehaan witnessed the most beautiful sight in the world. He saw Priya naked from the waist up. He was certain it was Priya, not from the size of her chest but from the lack of hair on her torso. To celebrate the moment, Jehaan did the one thing he shouldn't have—in that Fosbury Flop position, he began to bellow 'Caro Mio Ben' (My Own Dear One) with all his might. The powerful rendition caught Priya's attention and she turned and noticed the strange twisted form. She also noticed that the form had noticed her own distinctly superior form. By the end of the first verse of 'Caro Mio Ben',

Priya's heavenly orbs had been promptly replaced by Mr Godhwani's hairy ones.

Worse was to follow. The Hairy Beast wanted blood. Jehaan's parents and the whole colony were warned about a sex fiend, easily distinguishable from other sex fiends by his operatic voice. The boy's mind was more twisted than his body, The Beast informed all who cared to listen. Heartbroken, weeping and enraged, Jehaan's parents turned against him. Ashamed and alone, Jehaan blamed both his love of singing and his love of girls. He decided he had to give one up. After an intense emotional conflict, which lasted approximately four seconds, Jehaan gave up singing.

Gradually, Jehaan's creativity took a new turn. He channellized his energies into writing, especially poetry. His first line ever was, 'I used to know a girl called Priya.' Invariably, the poem would end with 'Unfortunately, Priya said "See ya."'

After graduating from college, Jehaan applied for a job as a trainee copywriter at D'Souza's. The advertising agency had a supremely successful formula. It copied the major European advertising campaigns and won many Indian awards. This noble practice is still in vogue today. Jehaan got the job with little difficulty, not because he gave a brilliant copy test (all he was asked to write was his full name), but because he was the only applicant in three and a half years.

Jehaan the Singer, Jehaan the Lover, and Jehaan the Poet had become an advertising writer. Or to be more precise, he was now Jehaan the Copier. It was at D'Souza's that he met his wife-to-be, Maria.

His days at D'Souza's were spent reading the four books kept in the agency library. The books included *Rajputs* by Henry Tod, *Lots of Rajputs* by Henry Tod, and the award-winning *Hell of a Lotta Rajputs*, also by Henry Tod. The fourth book, *Psychopathology of Everyday Life* by Sigmund Freud, had spent 29 years in the library without once being opened. It was on such a day at D'Souza's that Karl saw Maria for the first time. She had on a long skirt that may once have been a tablecloth and a pink T-shirt that had 'Boston Red Sox' emblazoned across it. Like most people in the subcontinent, Maria wore the T-shirt with pride blissfully unaware that the Red Sox were not really a pair of socks.

Jehaan couldn't believe his eyes when Samant, the Head of Media at D'Souza's, got to Maria first. The cheeky fellow had taken the lead of becoming 'first friend'. That was not a good sign. In all offices, in all cultures, across the world, a new person was shown around the office by someone known as the 'first friend'. The first friend would in all probability come to 'own' the new employee, almost turning the latter into the proverbial putty in his hands, and would feel licensed to do exactly as he chose with the person in question. Samant, the wily old fox, though excellent at his work, had one awful weakness. He couldn't resist anything in a skirt. That explained why his fourth marriage was crumbling. It also explained why he hadn't enjoyed his last holiday in Scotland.

Having established his rights as first friend, Samant showed Maria around the office. Something that normally took 27 seconds—D'Souza's comprised one large room surrounded on three sides by three cubicles—took over 43½ minutes, 30 of which were spent in Samant's own cubicle looking at pictures of Samant dressed as Samson, as Bhim, as Errol Flynn, and the one he was most proud of, Samant dressed vaguely as Samant. (Samant's modus operandi was simple, and once the women saw his get-ups and his variety, they were generally hooked. Soon afterward, they felt suitably encouraged to marry him.) It was then that Jehaan's wits came to his aid. He quietly interrupted Samant (who, for the moment, was showing Maria a picture of a male model in swimming trunks and passing it off as his younger self) and informed him that he had a phone call.

When Samant told him to take down a message, he responded with the three words that always sent a chill down Samant's spine. 'Mrs Samant.' Sounding like a man falling out of an aircraft, Samant asked, 'Which one?' The answer almost made him black out. 'Number three.' Jehaan had effectively delivered the coup de grâce. Samant left the room as if he were approaching the gallows, and Jehaan grabbed his opportunity.

Trying to sound erudite, Jehaan quoted Herman Melville's introductory line from *Moby Dick*, 'Call me Ishmael.' It was only when she began addressing him as Ishmael that Jehaan realized that it may not have been such a good idea.

Jehaan and Maria hit it off superbly after some initial teething trouble. There were a few things that Jehaan would often recount to her much later in their lives: the time he stepped on Maria's skirt in a crowded

9

restaurant as they were about to leave; or reversed his car on her foot while dropping her home from work; or took her to a shop and left her behind; or mistook her for her mother on the telephone—somethig no woman has enjoyed since Marc Antony mistook Cleo for her mother, at the precise moment she was exiting her bath.

Maria, Karl's mother, was the youngest of three siblings and as a child she had been very athletic. This made her rather unpopular as beating boys in flat races tends to do. When she started offering them a ten pace lead, they boycotted her completely. It was then that Maria learnt some very valuable lessons: (a) women are superior to men, (b) men are deeply conscious of this superiority, (c) if you rub men's noses in the dirt, they are bound to break down or cry and generally become inconsolable, and (d) men are hairy and it is advisable not to vacuum clean around them.

Maria was also very altruistic and helpful by nature. Who could forget the time she helped old Mrs Ranganathan to her feet after a car had hit her and sped off. Maria's father had been the driver, but of course that was a different matter altogether. It was her genuine compassion coupled with her good looks (in the ratio of about 1:9) that caused Jehaan Marshall to fall head over heels in love with her.

One fine day…awright, awright, who can quite recall the weather that day… one day anyway, Jehaan asked Maria out to lunch, which was normally pretty worrisome for Maria as Jehaan invariably ran out of money well before they ran out of lunch. So she quickly packed some extra cash in her little purse to save Jehaan some serious embarrassment later. At lunch, as they dug into their chilli chicken, chicken chowmein, and fried rice (by Union law, all Chinese restaurants must compulsorily serve these three dishes to validate their claim of serving authentic Chinese cuisine), Jehaan felt like singing. He actually felt like singing! He took a deep breath and then began slowly. As the other diners started running helter-skelter, Jehaan realized something was amiss. His singing voice had been dormant for so long that the soothing, mellifluous sound had been replaced by a grating, rusty, guttural growl. It was a cross between an Altaf Raja qawaali and the sound of two grizzly bears in an amorous engagement. Unique as this sound was, it was also rather frightening. Grown men cowered in fear, and the staff left the premises immediately.

Jehaan regained his poise in the empty restaurant and, clearing his voice, delivered Vivaldi's 'Les Quatre Saisons'. Halfway through the Allegro, he realized he wasn't a violin and that Maria's patience was wearing thin. Instead of impersonating instruments, which is only feasible if you are a five-year-old, he broke into some Western vocals with his own impression of the inimitable Richard Crooks. He sang 'Only a Rose' with great gusto, his now majestic tenor reverberating through the room. He did it standing on one leg as he felt that raising one leg always helped him hit the high notes. As he ended the song, he stamped both his feet like a man who'd just jumped off a ladder. Then, falling on one knee, he asked Maria if she would marry him.

But for Maria, first things came first. Holding one leg up and singing had given Jehaan a cramp. By kneeling, he had put the same leg under tremendous pressure. Even as his proposal reached its end, they both realized that standing up was out of the question. So Maria helped him roll on to his side. He then assumed the position a dog assumes when you tickle his stomach—lying on his back with all four paws in the air. Of course, two of Jehaan's paws had faded black shoes on.

As the blood slowly returned to Jehaan along with fragments of his dignity, he repeated the question, albeit sheepishly and almost to no one in particular, in case it remained unanswered. The answer caught him by surprise. Quite resigned to failure, and with rapidly failing self-esteem, the last thing Jehaan had expected was a 'yes'. In disbelief, he asked, 'Are you sure?' When she replied in the affirmative, the cramps hit him severely once again—this time in the other leg. Maria encouraged her husband-to-be to lie down in the empty diner.

This brings us to the most important moment of Karl Marshall's life. True, he was yet to be born. However, it is a fundamental scientific fact that if his parents had not wed, Karl wouldn't have been born. If he hadn't been born, he wouldn't have had life. If indeed he didn't have a life, this book would have never been written. Which means both you and I, dear reader, would have been saved a whole load of tripe but for this singularly important fact of Karl Marshall's life—his parents' wedding.

The wedding and the next few months passed

uneventfully, and four years and seven months later, the Marshalls gave birth. Okay, perhaps that's not quite right because try as he might Jehaan Marshall could not possibly have given birth. Although after nine months of his wife's mood swings, he really wished he were the one carrying the baby. The Marshalls' respective careers had entered a comfortable phase. Now in separate agencies, Maria was Vice President, Marketing, while Jehaan had completed reading his fifty-seventh book on Rajput history and tradition, without once succumbing to Freud.

On the fifth of August, 19… something or the other, Karl Marshall was born. At first, he was not much to look at. In fact, when it comes to babies, only parents and close relatives can actually see something worthwhile. For the rest, it's just another oversized ice-cream cone wrapped in a white napkin. Karl Marshall was handed to his father Jehaan in this same traditional uniform. Jehaan's first thought was that he'd better return it to the aquarium. Then, better sense prevailed. The aquarium would be closed that day; it was a Sunday. He tried to look for signs of life in the ice-cream cone. The eyes didn't even blink. Should he jab at the ice-cream, or make baby sounds? Jehaan did neither. Instead, he chose to unleash 'A'Vuchella' on the unsuspecting hospital floor, despite the signs plastered all over that indicated quite emphatically that this was a silent zone.

Jehaan was apprehended on the fourth line of 'A'Vuchella'. At first, one of the nurses tried to administer a tranquillizer as she could not identify from which orifice the cacophony was originating.

13

Two heavily pregnant mothers in adjacent rooms started to lactate. Amidst all the commotion, Karl Marshall opened his panic-stricken eyes. This was the same look he would use in the future as a regular and spontaneous reaction to his father's voice. Jehaan Marshall was escorted out of the hospital. Indignant and with a bruised ego, Jehaan vowed that he would never sing in public again. The world didn't deserve his voice. For once, Jehaan Marshall was right.

Reputed psychiatrists Dr Seiss and Dr Sukhinder, whose classic work *It's Better to Know Your Child than the Child You Know* still sells at bookstores, point out that a child's basic personality can be ascertained by day three. I tend to disagree, for me it was day four. In Karl Marshall's case, it seemed more like day 488. As a newborn, he was pretty expressionless, which is really saying something. Like most babies, he'd stare at you without blinking for hours on end, though why an adult might spend valuable time on a working day staring back at a newborn was a question only Jehaan could answer.

As Karl approached his eighteenth month, however, he acquired a certain maturity and sophistication. He now cried almost continuously. If his father wished him good morning, he'd respond by crying. When asked if he was hungry, he'd break down like Michael Jackson at a seniors' bash. If someone tried to hug him, he'd fall back on the floor, kick his legs in the air and sob inconsolably.

Crying wasn't the worst of his tantrums; it was just the beginning, a mere sideshow to the main feature which was presented only on special occasions. And what were these occasions, you ask? If, for example, a drop of water or any other liquid touched him, he flapped his hands like a young bird in flight school and bawled in a way the world had not seen since Columbus sailed for India, and realized that he had forgotten his TB shots before the voyage.

Karl's wails were like a classical concerto gone badly wrong. It was a progression consisting of four distinct gradations. Step 1 was a loud warning sound like the wind in the desert or wind stuck in an instrument or, well, er... just a violent wind. This eerie sound set the tone for the performance to come. Step 2 saw the upper body come into play. Hands flew in all directions, reminiscent of the early Bruce Lee, only deadlier. Step 3 saw the start of the lower body's involvement. Legs began flailing, knocking at humans and furniture alike with scud-like precision. The might of an eighteen-month-old baby is often underestimated, as many ashtrays, vases, and cabinets discovered. But all these steps paled in comparison to Step 4. In Step 4, a holistic approach was adopted. Combining the finer points of Ju-Jitsu, savate, karate, kung fu, and parliamentary behaviour, with the finesse and balance of Kuchipudi, Odissi, and Kathakali dance forms, Karl, all eighteen months of him, became a veritable machine of destruction. Step 4 found the Babynator targeting one specific spot and focusing exclusively on its total elimination. His victim could be as small as a leather shoe or as large as Mr and Mrs Parekh. In either case, the assault would be swift and lethal. Jehaan Marshall would never forget the sight of the Parekhs fleeing the scene like refugees in a rush, clinging to their tattered clothes and tattered pride, Mrs Parekh outrunning her husband as always.

The ultimate holiday in the Marshall household was Karl's birthday. Birthdays in India are vastly important, and children's birthdays are more important than ususal. Keep in mind that the average Indian male's childhood extends to the age of 44. Let's do a comparative study of an average two-year-old's birthday in Boston, against an average two-year-old's birthday in Mumbai.

For the Boston child, two sets of grandparents, the immediate family, and one neighbour are invited to the birthday party, which is held at the boy's house. Punch is served, cake is cut, and within 45 minutes the party concludes and all nine partygoers go their separate ways. Very often, one set of grandparents is already dead or, worse still, divorced, so the final tally of guests may actually be even lower. For the evening's entertainment, an elderly uncle may dress up as a donkey for a civilized session of 'pin the tail on the donkey', an old American pastime that originally evolved from a form of torture practised on Mexican prisoners who refused the poisonous staple diet of cheese sandwiches and apple pie. The two-year-old from Boston is usually dressed in a white short-sleeved shirt and oversized shorts with a cap and a bow tie. The boy says 'please' and 'thank you' to everyone and is quite relieved when the ordeal is over and tries never to mention his birthday again, until he is 32.

Now let's examine the Mumbai boy's birthday. The guest list includes all relatives. Remember that most Indian families number 220 by conservative estimates.

Then add the 75 members of the child's play school, all the residents from the building and adjoining buildings, all the father's colleagues from work, all the mother's acquaintances, all friends from the local club and their children, all staff members, and a few small-time celebrities to ensure press participation and a little publicity. A successful party translates into a newspaper photograph of the parents, the tiny tot, and Minor Celebrity No. 1074 holding a yellow teddy bear. The birthday party cannot be accommodated in the house; instead, a prominent club or restaurant is booked. Event organizers and professional party handlers take over. A variety entertainment show is put up. A master of ceremonies with an affected English accent (it is a fact universally acknowledged that if you place an Indian before a microphone, he immediately develops an affected English accent) then makes the kids play a variety of games, endemic to the urban Indian landscape, such as Passing the Parcel, London Statue, and Chinese Whispers. The evening's entertainment culminates in a puppet show that often follows a story designed to threaten the sanity of civilized men.

The spread normally includes about 27 dishes, and it is in the serving of the food that another strange and uniquely Indian phenomenon is observed. Unlike in Boston, the children present at the parties are accompanied by their governesses—the parents' presence notwithstanding—known in India by the less flattering title of 'ayah' or 'maid'. Bedecked in their partygoing finery, the maid community is usually in full attendance, looking like slimmer versions of the mothers themselves. The Mumbai boy's birthday party is, for all practical purposes, *their* party. They gossip and laugh and exchange empowering notes about one another's employers and their ill-gotten ways, but the phenomenon in question is witnessed only when the food is served. The maids descend on the buffet like Atilla the Hun's marauding elephants and, within minutes, all 27 dishes, hundreds of kilos and litres of food and drink have vanished. Such gluttony is unparalleled. Atilla's elephants laboured up mountains, their appetite was justified, and besides they were...er, elephants. But none can tell why Indian maids display such a colossal, almost vengeful appetite. At the end of the party, the fattened maids, parents, and children return home with a huge present each, given by the birthday boy. The cost of this 'reverse' present is normally three times the Boston father's monthly salary. It is inexplicable then that a Bostonian should be considered a member of the first world and a Mumbaikar an inhabitant of the third world. These labels ought to be banned immediately.

chapter 2

One of the saddest moments for a child is the day he discovers that life is not just about eating, pooping, and simultaneously making sounds from different orifices. Don't get me wrong, the latter action is truly a fine art and not every child can compose an equally stunning symphony. But one day, every child is rudely robbed of his simple, twin pleasures of 'food in' and 'food out'. This happens when he is introduced to that dreaded refugee camp for small people—school.

Everything was going swimmingly for young Karl. His workday began at 7 am and ended by 7:10 am when he had emptied himself publicly, as was his wont. As job descriptions go, it wasn't the most glamorous and sophisticated, but as they say, it was a job and a job's a job (no pun intended). When school replaced this this rigorous workday, Karl was shattered, and he experienced something that would happen to him subsequently each time he felt a little flustered. Karl began to feel as if he was underwater, and it was getting more and more difficult to breathe. It was only when his mother pulled his head up from inside the full tub that he realized that he had *actually* been underwater all the while. This was to become notorious as Karl's Ostrich Reaction to anything mildly traumatic, which at that stage included all activities outside his three chosen areas of expertise: (a) pooping, (b) sleeping, and (c) eating, often performed in that order. Neither was it Karl's fault alone that his basic introduction to school went quite wrong.

Until then, Karl had been used to a very simple style of clothing, which basically comprised his three fingers around his central stations and not much else. White shirts and blue shorts were another matter. I mean, why do all schools have the same uniform in all corners of our globe—white shirts and blue shorts? Honestly, they take the 'one world' idea a little too far. In Germany, it's white shirts and blue shorts, in Rwanda it's white shirts and blue shorts, in Scotland—there's a twist here—white shirts and blue skirts. But wherever you look, it's white and blue. Returning to Karl's preparation for his first day at school, a white shirt was suddenly thrust upon him by four adult hands. Karl immediately faced the usual problems—the collar was too tight, the pants were too long and tended to fall off every time he went on all fours, and, worst of all (and in this there is a lesson for all kid apparel manufacturers), the dreaded tag made its presence felt right away. Now let's spend a few minutes examining this specimen—the tag.

It is normally rectangular in shape and protrudes forward at a 90-degree angle. Placed at the back but on the inside of the shirt, it tends to irritate one much more than Rakhi Sawant does. Often this irritation leads to a child's absolute psychological disintegration. But why do apparel manufacturers persist with this menace? Elementary, my dear reader. All clothing makers, big or small, from any corner of the earth, are childless, i.e., these uniform makers have no children, do not live in close proximity to children, have never heard of children, and may not be fully convinced that children really exist. This also explains why they live to an average age of 96½, and rarely experience the joy of herpes.

As Karl's shorts swallowed his body, his father quoted liberally from *Hamlet*, 'Costly thy habit as thy purse can buy, but not expressed in fancy, rich not gaudy, for the apparel oft proclaims the man.' Karl vomited in response. Ironically, that was exactly how the audience had reacted when *Hamlet* was first staged in England.

One of the other myths propagated by the West and exported to India is the myth of 'pre-school'. Let's get one thing straight—there is no such thing as a pre-school. A pre-school is just the same as school, only it starts with a 'P'. A bit like how 'psychology' is the same as 'sycology' or 'pneumonia' is the same as 'neumonia' or 'know' is the same as 'knot'…er, maybe not.

By sending your child to pre-school, you are actually just sending him to a school with different timings. Karl's first day in school, or pre-school, or whatever it is, was an eye opener. He was kept in a room with other kids, toys were provided, and nursery rhymes played in the background. So far, so good. In fact, Karl actually started enjoying himself and soon became the centre of attraction with his remarkable dance performance.

Just as the other kids had gathered around him, Karl began to feel a certain dampness. As it became apparent he had involuntarily relieved himself, the spot on his shorts became the cynosure of sixteen other eyes, each belonging to a trained, crack marksman who could tell the difference between a wet spot caused by a bodily fluid, and one caused by an external source. As the applause turned to laughter, and the laughter to jeers, Karl turned and fled. However, he was trapped and as Ms Mulla tried to help him repair the damage, he hid behind a chair. For an infant, there is no comeback from 'Public Wet-patch Display' (PWD). Many children become scarred for life. A few exceptions like Adolf Hitler, Napoleon Bonaparte, and Michael Jackson, turn humiliation into powerful negative energy, but in most cases, PWD leaves, er...if you'll forgive me, a lasting impression.

The next day, Karl refused to go to school. His parents tried all the usual ruses—the entire family walked around with patches, or showed Karl pictures of famous men with wet patches, and even went to a swimming pool where the guy with the dry patch was the odd one out. Nothing worked. Then, finally, after four days of sitting at home, Karl resumed his education. Now it seemed not everything about pre-school was so terrible as Karl had thought initially. It was on the day he resumed school that he met Kunal.

The class itself was a little yellow room. Classes all over India are held in little yellow rooms. They seem to be a prerequisite for a good education. The teachers may not have degrees, the school may lack basic stationery and infrastructure, but it must have a little

22

yellow room. As long as a class was conducted in one of these, education continued uninterrupted.

Karl's class had a total of nine children. Okay, eight children and one really small man with a moustache. Jayant Godhwani was a lovely boy…er, man…er, boy. However, Jayant was one of those rare specimens who had 'haired' early like his grandfather before him. Now a child with this condition is subject to much scrutiny from all and sundry. On the first Parents' Day in school, not one but at least seven different sets of parents mistakenly asked the four-year-old Jayant if his son was in the same class as theirs. As a result, Jayant was the only child in school who insisted on wearing long-sleeved shirts and trousers, perhaps to pass himself off as a middle school student. On his fifth birthday, even the principal couldn't control her peals of laughter as she wished him 'Happy Fifth Birthday!'

Let's leave Jayant alone for a second and turn our attention to a portly figure in Karl's class called Kunal. Kunal, quite simply, looked like an orange. If you carefully observe an unpeeled orange, you will realize it is one whole body, without any divisions. It's just one continuous stream of orange plasma. Kunal's shape was similar. His round head slipped right into his round torso, which conveniently overshadowed the spindly legs at the bottom. Effectively, from certain angles, all you saw from bottom to top were a few toes peeping out from under a cylindrical object. In other words, you had a human orange. Of course, it was only later that he transformed into a lollipop but at the time, Kunal was all orange.

Kunal was a shy, demure orange who kept to himself. Not being particularly social and being extremely withdrawn, the teaching staff encouraged him to sit next to Karl, who was just the opposite. Karl couldn't sit still, he couldn't keep quiet, and he loved to participate in any group activity. If a question was asked in class, Karl's hand would automatically shoot up regardless of whether he knew the answer or not. This led to Karl becoming a master at the 'winging it' style of group participation, in which the only rule you follow is that you must never actually know anything about the subject on which you are speaking. The technique has been perfected by parliamentarians across the world.

Initially, Karl was unhappy to have an orange sitting beside him. He had been quite satisfied with his previous partner, Shefali. In many ways, Shefali was Karl's first fan. She giggled at everything he did and always allowed him to take the lead. If he raised his hand, Shefali would go 'Miss, miss, miss' to help direct the teacher's attention towards him. Karl and Shefali took their relationship to another level—the level of physical intimacy. This was done through the traditional act of rubbing elbows.

When Shefali was displaced, Karl didn't take kindly to the newcomer. Nobody quite likes a hot young girl being replaced by an orange, and as Karl told somebody later on, 'You can't actually rub elbows with an orange because an orange doesn't really have any elbows.'

Whoever said all children are innocent? Kunal's class was full of such innocents, and he was the one they all picked on. During the break, when the teacher's supervision was at its poorest, the children started playing a variety of games. Rejecting perennial favourites like Catch n' Cook and Chor Police, they opted for more innovative games. The three most popular and most frequently repeated games were Pulling Kunal's Hair, Tickling Kunal's Tummy, and Stomping on Fallen Kunal. As the kids matured, the games became progressively more sophisticated, and you initially pulled Kunal's hair, then proceeded to tickle his tummy, and then with true childish chivalry, ended the session by stomping on the poor fellow till you exhausted yourselves, or a teacher noticed the commotion.

It was during one such game that a strange thing happened. Carl Jung, in his two-pronged observation of children, said: 'Children are both very short and very competitive.' Of course, this is a rough translation from the original German so a few key words have had to be replaced. The point, however, is that kids are, have always been, and will always be highly competitive...and a little short. So one day, while indulging in a cerebral round of Kunal Jousting, one of the other kids mistakenly stepped on Karl's hands instead of Kunal's unprotected back. This changed the dynamics of the game as Karl set upon the errant foot. Soon, the whole class turned on the errant child and he soon replaced Kunal in that vastly popular game. In the mêlée that followed, Kunal crawled to safety at his usual urgent speed, roughly equivalent to that of an adolescent caterpillar.

After the teacher broke up the bunch, Kunal, mistakenly thinking that Karl had received a heart transplant and had voluntarily protected him, went up to his hero to offer his thanks. Although the power of habit and conditioning compelled Karl to start pulling Kunal's hair and tickling him, Kunal persisted with his thanks. This led to Karl pulling Kunal's hair less and less over time, and eventually it died out altogether. It must be added though that Kunal began to wear a cap for a little protection, a habit that continued into his early adulthood, which for Kunal, unlike Karl, started when he was eight years old.

As they progressed from class to class, Kunal and Karl gradually became very close friends, Kunal mistakenly basing their friendship on his notion of Karl as his protector. For Karl, the relationship was based on a far higher, nobler calling—lunch. Kunal was one of the few kids who got a lot of lunch. Unlike Karl's boring sandwiches, Kunal's lunch was brought exactly one minute before lunchtime by his domestic help, Manju. Thanks to Manju's unusual figure and posture, Kunal's tiffin could be spotted approaching the school gate from miles away. You see, the 79-year-old Manju's torso always remained bent over and her behind protruded well above her head. This gave her a distinctive 'M' shape. Many of the other children's tiffinwalas took advantage of this and often rested their tiffin carriers on her back or behind as they waited for the lunch bell to ring.

Two incidents are worth dwelling on—two incidents that cemented the friendship between the two youngsters.

The first incident came to be known as the Karate Incident. At about the time the boys were ten years old, karate had begun becoming very popular in cities. Soon, the two friends enrolled in a karate class. As part of the warm-up exercises, they were asked to perform ten push-ups. Most managed this effortlessly. Kunal, however, transformed this traditional exercise into an art form. He took the basic philosophy of the push-up—which is to push your body away from the floor intensely and as many times as possible—and reversed it. Instead of pushing the torso up repeatedly, he would sink to the floor and remain motionless. The 'push-down' was Kunal's first but not last contribution to physical exercise. Soon, the whole class adopted this new style. Instead of twenty push-ups, the kids were doing one push-down for twenty seconds. In no time at all, the sensei found himself tearing his hair in frustration, as the karate class seemed to have lost its meaning.

The invention of the push-down catalyzed creativity, creativity born from that underrated but rare virtue, absolute laziness. Karl in turn came up with the Great Indian Nose Trick, where he'd gradually but successfully shove three fingers into one nostril. It caught on like wildfire. Even talent competitions were not spared. 'Ladies and gentlemen, Richa Bhatia will sing "Autumn Leaves" followed by Rakesh Puri who will attempt to put three fingers into one nostril simultaneously.'

The sensei made a last-ditch attempt to salvage his class by showing them one of those Hong Kong martial arts flicks that were always made in seven days. This one was called *The Scorpion on the Tiger's Tooth*. Sadly, they were fifteen minutes into the movie and the room was empty, primarily because there was no sign of a scorpion or a tiger anywhere. The only thing that came of the film was that for the next four days the children all spoke with the same Chinese English accents. In fact, the Great Indian Nose Trick followed by some commentary in a Chinese English accent became a big hit and was a 'must-be-seen' at all birthday parties and large gatherings. As for the poor sensei, one innocuous push-down had ruined him. He soon closed the karate class and took up plumbing, an act that unkind observers attributed to a latent reverence for the Great Indian Nose Trick.

The karate incident elevated the two boys to cult status. Other boys were drawn to the almost otherworldly power of their talent. In fact, just like Julius Caesar and Napoleon before them, the two were accorded a distinct form of greeting which involved the person acknowledging them touching the tip of his nose with three fingers. Caesar used to get the 'arc', Napoleon a prolonged salute, Kunal and Karl got the three-finger salute. Girls also seemed drawn to them, proving that given the right time and circumstances, three fingers in the nose could become a far more popular and mesmerizing art form than Odissi dancing, Hindustani classical singing, or even Carnatic vocals, none of which interested the two boys whatsoever.

The second incident that cemented their friendship involved a boy called Meherdod Marfatia. It involved four dangerous things that are innocent enough in isolation, but when combined can be more lethal than a Britney Spears outfit. These four things are hockey sticks, an open field, eleven-year-old boys, and chewing gum.

Both Karl and Kunal liked to chew gum. In itself, this is unremarkable. Lots of living beings like to chew gum—Viv Richards, Kobe Bryant, cows—to give just three examples. But Karl and Kunal had only just discovered the joys of chewing gum—it seemed to mark a coming of age, the end of the boiled sweets era, and the possibility of a range of secondary activities such as pasting gum under friends' desks, on seats, on bag handles, on door handles, and most popularly, in hair.

On that fateful day, an inter-class hockey match was in progress. Karl was at the centre of action, while Kunal was doing what he did best—pretending. While the two rival classes were at each other's throats, Kunal was doing his bit to fool the staff into thinking that he was actually playing. He did this by alternately moving two feet in either direction and dropping and picking up his stick every few minutes. Suddenly, a fight broke out mid-field between Karl and Meherdod Marfatia. Marfatia was the smallest, shortest boy on the field, about four inches shorter than his hockey stick. Karl, as a rule, followed the military diktat of the great General Yang Yang (who may or may not have been the great badminton champion of the 1980s) who once said, 'Always, always pick a fight with someone smaller, shorter, and weaker than yourself.' This is the noblest act conceivable in martial life. Only in exceptional circumstances may you abandon this diktat. What are those circumstances? In the event you find someone even smaller, shorter, and weaker than

29

your original choice. Then you may abandon Attack A and switch to the relatively minor Attack B.

Karl had dribbled a ball on to the oncoming defender Meherdod's ankle. The result was a resounding thud, Marfatia abused Karl, and Karl decided to use the most deadly weapon in his arsenal— chewing gum in the opponent's hair. An already enraged Marfatia drew himself up to his full height, which really was a waste of time because nobody took any notice. Marfatia swished his stick around, aiming a blow at Karl's head. Behind him, however, lurked the hunched figure of the world's worst hockey player since Pavarotti tried his hand at the game—Kunal. Kunal was in his trying-to-find-my-hockey-stick position, when Marfatia's stick found him.

Marfatia's trial and subsequent sentencing was conducted by the Physical Education teacher, Mr Airuban Das. Here is the exact text of that trial.

'Marfatia, silly boy, stupid maroon [that was Das saying 'moron' in his Bengali accent], you hit Kunal with your stick?'

Now, this was a rhetorical question Marfatia was not supposed to answer. Sadly, Marfatia's limited growth was not restricted to height alone.

Marfatia: Sir, I didn't do anything...

Das: Silly boy. Stupid maroon. Lying to me? Lying to Mr Das?

Again, this was rhetorical, and when Das spoke in the third person, it was always a bad omen.

Marfatia: Sir, actually Karl hit me...

Das: Lying to me, lying to Mr Das? Am I a maroon? Is Das a maroon? Go for twenty rounds.

Marfatia: I don't know that, but I didn't start it.

Das: Arguing with Das, go for 20,000 rounds.

Marfatia: Sir, how can I possibly run 20,000 rounds of the ground?

Das: Still arguing with Das, silly boy, maroon, go for 20 million rounds.

Till today, students of the school wonder if Mafartia is still trying to complete his punishment.

Studies took on a whole new meaning as the boys reached the ninth and tenth standards. This was Mumbai in the late 1980s. A time when places to stay, parking spots, and Parsis were all being threatened with extinction. Many upmarket children began developing a back pain because of the thousands of books they were asked to carry day in and day out. Young Kunal felt the pain doubly as he often carried Karl's books. It was around this time that Kunal earned his teenage sobriquet, 'Quarter'. This nickname stuck until he reached college. This story is worth repeating in many languages. Thankfully this writer is well versed in barely one.

The scene was the chemistry class. Mr Verma (who had a unique way of communicating by never opening his mouth wider than half an inch) was vaguely in charge. On this particular day, Verma opened his mouth even less than his usual half inch. This was a sure sign that he would start a new chapter or had forgotten his medication and was soon going to hyperventilate. Unfortunately for Karl and Kunal, this time it was the former. The new chapter was about valency. After a futile fifteen minutes spent failing to convince the class that valency was not in fact a city

31

in Spain, Verma continued with his lecture, facing the blackboard for most of his discourse. At the end of the one-sided performance, which even the blackboard struggled to understand, he handed the boys a sheet of paper containing a valency balance sheet. For those of you who don't know what a valency balance sheet is, here is my short explanation—I have no idea. Further, I've made it an uncompromising habit never to associate with those who associate themselves with valency balance sheets, even if they are Spanish. We must now move on to the next day, not because nothing untoward happened that evening but because we have no idea what happened to Mr Verma for the rest of that day. The next one, however, told another story.

As the class gathered for the chemistry lesson, Mr Verma announced a pop test on…valency. Being young, sincere, dedicated, hard-working students, nobody in their right mind had even glanced at yesterday's valency sheet, other than Arvind Rungta and Tanvi Mehta. Note though that Arvind and Tanvi were the kind of students who memorized menus in restaurants on their off days.

The test was a disaster with most of the class failing. Nine out of 50 seemed like the average score, so Karl was delighted to receive his double-digit glory of eleven. Then, Mr Verma, always fond of his Churchillian references, said, 'Never in the history of chemistry was so little scored by so many at the same time, but even out of the little, one name has covered itself with honour. Kunal, step forward. It gives me great pride and joy to announce that you have scored the lowest score I have ever witnessed in my 27-year-long teaching career. Half on fifty. That is 0.5 out of 50. Half of one out of fifty. Not even making it to a single digit. What do you have to say while accepting your honour?'

Kunal who by now had come some way from being that shy, introverted boy and was known to have quite a well-rounded personality, both literally and figuratively, spoke up.

'Sir, can you round off my half to one?' he asked matter-of-factly.

The class was tense and expectant. And then occurred one of those unforgettable moments that seem to make the entire educational process worth its while. Mr Verma rose with dignity and said, 'That's impossible, Mr Kunal. You see, I've already rounded off your marks to half from a quarter.'

As one would expect from any civilized, evolved people, Kunal received a standing ovation. Many of those students today have forgotten every single lesson they were taught in school, but all can recall quite clearly where they were and what they were doing when Kunal got a quarter of a mark out of 50. It became the single greatest achievement of Karl's generation and granted Kunal immortality, with future generations speaking in awe of how they knew a boy whose elder brother had a neighbour whose friend rode in the same bus as the boy who scored a quarter of one mark. Kunal and Mr Verma became part of popular folklore, much like Gary Sobers and Malcolm Nash.

The one thing Karl craved as a young boy was a

canine companion. In the *Arthashastra*, Kautilya, also known as Chanakya, had said there are three phases in a male's life. In the first he craves a canine companion, in the second he craves a female companion (not necessarily canine), and in the third phase he craves for the canine companion to return and bite the female companion.

Finally, after much pleading and begging and threatening to go on a hunger strike, which was actually encouraged by both his parents, Jehaan got Karl a racially integrated black-and-white pup whom they named after the world's greatest singer, Enrico Caruso. Rico was a bright, chirpy puppy who was more than happy to be a part of the Marshall household. He showed his gratitude by ripping apart Maria's sarees and dresses, all of Jehaan's shoes, most of Karl's toys, all of his friends, and finally the curtains, the towels, and the left front leg of all the chairs. With this last act, he displayed a political leaning that would soon become less and less popular in the new India, even in its last bastions of Kerala and Kolkata.

The Marshall family rallied around the new addition despite these minor glitches. Generously, Jehaan offered to do all the dog walking, nobly allowing Maria to handle the grooming. Grooming a puppy involves three routine activities: cleaning his pee, cleaning his poop, and cleaning him after his pee and his poop.

It was during Enrico Caruso's early years that the bonding between father, son, and the holy dog was at its best.

Every morning at 6 am, Jehaan would take Karl

and Enrico Caruso to the nearby Hanging Gardens. The Hanging Gardens ostensibly got its name from the gallows that operated there many years ago and offered cheap entertainment, but for the Marshalls it got its name from the riff-raff that could be seen hanging around in it at any time of day. Now by 'riff-raff' Jehaan clearly meant anyone who came dog-less to the garden. This was roughly 97.5 per cent of the population.

On day one, Jehaan decided to share his tremendous animal expertise and knowledge (largely gleaned by watching the movie *Paws Claws Jaws* twice as a teenager) with young Karl.

First came a performance of Fetch the Ball. Here, Jehaan would throw a tennis ball a few yards away and then loudly request Enrico Caruso to fetch it. This gruff request soon turned into a polite plea and finally degenerated into Jehaan desperately begging Enrico Caruso for a response. The German Beagle, however, is a different sort of dog. In fact, there is plenty of evidence to prove he isn't really a dog and is, in all probability, a cat disguised as a dog. If you want a dog to respond to orders, go for a German Shepherd or a Doberman Pinscher, but definitely not a German Beagle who is known to take no notice of a trainer or a curt command, let alone an impassioned plea on bended knee at six in the morning. Jehaan, however, wouldn't let the matter rest.

After a seventh consecutive futile throw, he turned and grabbed his son's shoulders. 'Son, now watch and learn. With a young pup, you must work out the social dynamics right at the start. He must know who's boss. A couple of passers-by are laughing at me thinking the dog is not responding to training, but I'm going to show you how persistence pays. With a puppy, as with people, you must be firm, gentle, and above all persistent to get results.'

He then proceeded to do something very strange. After flinging the ball and barking a few quick futile commands to fetch, he, a 44-year-old man in a clean pair of trousers and creaseless shirt, dropped down on all fours and followed the ball. Upon reaching the ball, Jehaan proceeded to pick it up with his mouth, and returned to the starting line on all fours.

Enrico Caruso was not impressed. He gave Karl a strange look. A look that was part sardonic and part nonchalant. Karl looked on in horror. He quickly counted eight key witnesses to the event. The first was the Sharmas' domestic worker Bharat who was a known gossip and embellisher of facts. The Kapoors with their Labrador were in splits. Mr Surender Kapoor was laughing so much his shirt button popped open, and Karl got the distinct feeling that the Kapoors' Labrador Ginny was laughing too. Jehaan for his part wore a smug and triumphant look; he was sure he had connected with Enrico Caruso in a way a man rarely ever connects with a dog. He was right of course, but not in quite the way that he thought. Worse was to follow.

Jehaan insisted on letting Enrico Caruso off his leash. Karl was told not to worry as dogs instinctively followed the pack. Soon, a search party was launched to find the missing Beagle puppy. Ironically, it was Mr Surender Kapoor who found Enrico Caruso about half a kilometre away. By then Kapoor had laughed so much that all his buttons had popped open. As he handed the unfazed puppy to Karl, he said with a twinkle in his eye, 'You boys come back tomorrow okay, and, er... don't forget the tennis ball!' Completing his sentence with great difficulty, he broke into a grunt, which soon burst into uncontrollable laughter.

Karl decided then that enough was enough. He carried Enrico Caruso back home, ignoring all his father's pleas to let the puppy walk on his own. Round one to Enrico Caruso. Pretty soon everyone knew who the boss was.

As Karl enjoyed the new addition to their family, Kunal too decided that life needed to be made more interesting. His addition to his present existence was the common everyday cigarette. Kunal's father was a professional smoker. A professional smoker, as defined in the *Smokers' Almanac* of 1983, is one 'whose greatest talent is smoking', and his ability to smoke at any place and any time is what sets him apart from other people. In fact, Kunal Senior was proud of his college record of fourteen cigarettes smoked in 60 minutes. Those were the days before India's Cricket World Cup wins, tennis wins, and occasional Olympic glory, so Kunal Senior's achievement was definitely considered a legitimate sporting achievement and not something to be scoffed at.

Kunal Senior worked as a radio announcer and voiceover artist, and had a unique broadcasting style. Mid-sentence, he would break into a prolonged coughing fit (with an average duration of seventeen seconds), and often deem it below his dignity to complete his sentence. For instance, he'd start with 'Happy Birthday to Maria, from…cough, cough, breathe, cough, cough, breathe, cough, grunt, breathe heavily, wheeze… and now our next song on the play list is…Congratulations.'

Like many adolescent males, Kunal Junior idolized his father. And just as many sons want to be pilots, lawyers, or doctors like their fathers before them, Kunal wanted to be a cougher. He had in the past tried to include a put-on cough in conversation, but no one would pay him any heed, as a put-on cough is amongst the worst pieces of theatre imaginable. He decided then that the time had come for him to fulfil his father's expectations by having his first smoke.

It was while pillaging his father's cupboard that he saw it. Poets have waxed eloquent about it, philosophers and artists have been intoxicated by it, elder statesmen have gone to war over it. Nothing can compare to the sensation one experiences upon one's first sight of pornography. No summer breeze, no newborn baby, no first leaf of spring or snow-capped peak holds a candle to the sheer joy and beauty of pornography. There in Kunal's father's closet, right next to a carton of 555 cigarettes, was the greatest piece of literature Kunal had ever set eyes on. *Hustler* magazine for its part doesn't like leaving anything to the readers' imagination. Their principle is simple—if you've paid a large amount for the magazine, it's only morally right for the magazine to do all the work and for you to passively enjoy their work. Karl devoured the magazine like a silverback gorilla in heat. The entire carton of 555 lay nearby, having little impact and being completely overshadowed by the pristine beauty that is nakedness upon more gut-wrenching nakedness. Kunal decided he had to share his happiness. He put the magazine in a plastic bag and rushed to his friend's house.

Pornography, which is often likened to gold, can lead to conflict. Both boys fought over custody of the magazine. However, thanks to *Hustler*, they also learnt discipline and teamwork. Karl was custodian from 7 am to 1 pm, after which the magazine became Kunal's property. By 6 pm every evening, it had to be returned to the vault, well before Kunal Senior might find his treasure missing.

Access to pornography placed a great deal of responsibility upon Karl and Kunal. It immediately elevated the two to the apex of their circle at school, and they became the alpha males, so to speak. The perks of this privileged position of leadership were soon made abundantly clear. No longer did they have to carry their own bags; lunch boxes were offered to them first; and the concept of homework ceased to exist for them. Matters were put before them for settlement, and if the teacher asked the collective a question, perhaps about which chapter they should read, the whole class would turn and look to them for their decision. In return, the boys were allowed a few seconds with the magazine.

As their collection of pornographic magazines grew, Karl and Kunal realized they weren't just interested in the strangers in the magazines but also in actual, specific girls in their class. Karl chose the buxom Serena, Kunal opted for the staid but quietly pretty

Priya. Now that they lorded it over the boys, vassals were dispatched to Serena and Priya. The girls suddenly found their bags being carried, meals were offered to them, and they also received a stream of offers of homework completed and returned. While they didn't mind the first two, they realized that accepting help with their homework from a boy was unwise. The boys sensed this, and focused more on the bags and food.

In a class of 30, word about someone liking someone else gets out rather fast. In this case, it took four seconds. Considering the status of the two boys, the de facto President and Vice President of the class, the girls were quite tickled by the idea. Soon, the emissary headed back to the court of King Karl—this court was located about a foot behind the desk of Serena—with word that conditions were indeed favourable. And so with the connivance of about 25 people in the class, the first class romance took off.

As a young boy, Karl's interest in girls ranked just below his interest in the various hues of the monitor lizard and just above his interest in the textile prints of the 1940s. But the moment Karl set eyes on Miss January in his first *Hustler* magazine, two thoughts occurred to him simultaneously. The first was that girls must replace maths and science in his curriculum forthwith and, second (and this made him weep inconsolably for months), why couldn't there have been more than twelve months in a year? The calendar he concluded could only have been designed by a woman. Of course Karl did not realize then that he had just had his first *sexual* and *sexist* thought.

So taken in were the boys with the new subject that studies suddenly became even more dreary than usual. One look at Miss January's ample bosom (which in a rare act of nature actually grew bigger between pages 23 and 27) and all his academic queries seemed to evaporate. Okay, I'm lying, there still were several academic questions, but simply more relevant ones, such as: could Wendy Whopper really be her Christian name? If so then what were the Whoppers like…er… at home? Did she really only wear shoelaces all the time? And could gardening, sunbathing, and shopping actually be considered occupations? Little did Karl know that he was coming down with a disease that plagues most men—'an interest in sexitis'. What he also didn't know was that as he grew older, his interest in sexitis would mutate and spread into its more dangerous forms such as 'deeply frustrated at not getting it-itis', or its equally dangerous twin, 'Tysonitis'.*

Sexual imagery, fantasies and a more explicit language now dominated their thoughts as they learnt to appreciate the female form. Natasha, for one, they realized was not just a 'brain' but also a pair of beautiful legs. And when Tanya Singh ran, the entire male population watched unblinkingly. In Tanya's school diary, Marfatia commented that he hoped to see her on a 'thread mill'. It may have helped his case had he been able to spell 'treadmill' correctly.

As far as Serena and Priya were concerned, Karl and Kunal soon realized that due to some cruel twist

*The Indian version, 'Shakti Kapooritis', is still being investigated.

41

of fate, women don't exactly think like men. Strangely, they aren't as impressed by the reverse ice-cream trick, the push-down exercise over its more ingenious cousins, fingers in the underwear, or burping the alphabet in Hindi. They wanted to discuss *things*. This last statement astonished the two boys. What, after all, are 'things'? When they asked the ladies for further clarification, they were given the rejoinder, 'Stuff.' What the hell is 'stuff'? What the hell are 'things'? How the hell is 'stuff' related to 'things'? The two young lovers agonized over these questions. Nonetheless, they simply had to get closer to Priya and Serena. The two boys compiled a list of topics that might fall under the purview of 'things' and 'stuff'. The list included shoes, socks, more shoes, plants, hair, more shoes, animals, more shoes, more plants, and more animals.

Just when fate was beginning to seem utterly indifferent, something happened that tilted the balance a little in their favour—school gave over for the summer holidays. Karl and Kunal were not going to take it easy during the vacations this time, for they had a mission and... er...sort-of girlfriends.

On the positive side, they had passion, energy, and focus; simply put, they were in a permanent state of arousal. On the negative side, they didn't quite know how to channellize this state of arousal to everybody's benefit.

Hustler, Playboy, Penthouse, Mayfair, and *Human Digest* were unable to present a balanced view of the matter. The women in these magazines were all depicted in the noble act of removing their clothes.

This was very different from Serena and Priya, who would never come to the door in just their socks or bend provocatively over coffee tables for no apparent reason.

It was Kunal who came up with the idea of leaving a *Penthouse* magazine lying around. After all, if the girls only picked up the magazine and glanced through it, they would see the error of their ways and learn from their betters the correct modes of behaviour, etiquette, and dress sense. Normally Karl never plunged head first into a Kunal plan, but intoxicated with the possibility of success, and seething with sexual arousal, he decided to go along with it.

When he heard Serena's yell of disgust followed by Priya's shriek and departure from the room, Karl's high spirits evaporated for the first time in nine days. Kunal tried to salvage the situation by lamely passing the buck, 'It's not my mag, it's my dad's. He's a collector, he's got about 27 of these in his cupboard.'

Convinced now that not only the son but even the father was some sort of sexual fiend, the two girls threatened to take their business elsewhere. For a week, disaster seemed imminent. Wendy Whopper had let them down badly. Kunal had a good mind to shoot off a letter to the editor, but Karl reminded him that the particular issue was eleven years old.

Karl learnt three valuable lessons that summer: (a) what goes up must come down, (b) Boyle's law of flotation or how to clear your drain, and (c) if you try too hard, you'll always fail. The two boys decided that since they had no time for lesson (a) and couldn't really fathom lesson (b), as they had never met Boyle in their life, they would concentrate instead on lesson (c).

They relaxed, let go, and restarted with the girls. The odd movie, a walk, a shared cold drink, and suddenly it looked like God might be subscribing to *Hustler* after all. On Marine Drive, there operated a juicewala—quite possibly a crorepati—who had made his millions using only three square feet of a rent-free public pavement to ply his trade. Thousands drank at this juice stall every day. Some even returned. The only problem that customers encountered was in the ordering. Was it 'Two mango juice and three pineapple juices' or was it 'Two mango juices and three pineapple juice please'?

It was while discussing this vexing singular–plural problem that Karl felt a worm crawl up his right hand. His first reaction was to slap at it, and then stamp on it. But he realized, in the nick of time, that it wasn't really a worm or even a spider but was in fact Serena's smooth hand that had helped itself on to his. Karl battled vainly to wipe all thoughts of Wendy Whopper from his mind. If he lost control at this point, the summer of sex would die an instant death. By then, Fate in the shape of the buxom Serena had taken control.

On the long walk along Marine Drive, a most romantic setting, privy to arguably the dirtiest sea in the world, Karl felt a wet swab in his mouth. Years later he realized that the swab had been Serena's tongue. Karl and Serena became the 4,73,88,684th couple to kiss on Marine Drive. Had all these couples been fined the princely sum of five rupees each, India would have been the richest country in the world.

Karl's first attempt at kissing, like that of all sexually charged Indian males, was pathetic. With experience, of course, the kissing was to only get worse. That lovely afternoon on Marine Drive, a mere novice helped along only by Wendy Whopper, Karl made a serious effort to hold on to Serena's tongue once it had entered Fort Marshall.

Subconsciously, he recalled how whales offered their tongues to the killer whale, the orca, as an act of submission, hoping that the orca would spare their lives. Serena's tongue proved to be more elusive than *The Scarlet Pimpernel* on LSD. Every time he made a grab at it, it dipped away. The infernal tongue seemed to have a mind of its own. After ten attempts, Karl gave up and practised touching the roof of his own mouth with his own tongue instead. After what seemed like ages, Serena removed her tongue, and each tongue returned to its rightful owner. As they continued their walk, Karl, now feeling 10 feet 3 inches tall, made a few mental notes. He was now the new King of Marine Drive. He had just declared the summer of sex open. One rule though—no tongue. Yup, definitely no more tongue. Oh and a silent thank you to his friend, philosopher, and guide, Wendy Whopper.

The summer of sex also ushered in a new instrument, an instrument that would henceforth become integral to all their lives. The telephone! The telephone was to have a huge impact on India in the 1980s, comparable to that of the saree in the 1960s, or the wheel in the 1950s. It became an additional member of the highly populous, already overextended Indian joint family, and it also became the most popular. You see, whatever a family's dynamics (A may not be talking to B, or C and D might never eat together), all family members would talk to the telephone, and the telephone would occasionally talk back.

Karl and Kunal had initially used the telephone to talk to each other. Their conversations were normally loud and gregarious, and included four recurring topics: bodily fluids, parts of the female anatomy, sports, and more bodily fluids. Their parents watched in amazement as the boys discussed a single topic for more than three hours without a break. Whether it was classmate Mohan Desai's extra nipple or Bhairav Jathana's hairy back, flaws and features were systematically dissected over the telephone. Conversations were occasionally interspersed with loud laughter, heavy scratching, and carnal sounds.

But when the two boys started to talk to Serena and Priya on the phone, all that changed. Their tones were hushed. Previously loud conversations could no longer be picked up by the human ear. In fact when young boys talk to girls on the phone, they tend to follow certain unwritten rules. They turn their back to other family members, speak at the decibel level of ants (the smaller red ones), keep their head and chin down, and sustain this position and speech pattern for the next seventeen and a half hours or so, which is the average length of a conversation.

The Marshalls tried to deal with this new disturbance in an assured, mature way. They hid the phone. But when Karl threatened to invite Kunal and the girls over every day, they gave in out of sheer terror. So the summer passed with phone conversations, walks, and

God's greatest gift to mankind after the Pizza Neapolitano—girls.

In school, the good usually comes with the bad. After the holidays, school resumed with exams. The latter are a severe intrusion into one's love life and telephone time. They are an unnecessary hindrance and may be thought to be the fourth worst menace plaguing our world after nuclear proliferation, ethnic and religious violence, and modern jazz. No one has yet understood their purpose. Karl often spent hours pondering who invented exams. Where did he stay? Was he heavily intoxicated or clinically insane at the time of invention? They are an effective means of torture in urban India, compelling normal children to stop thinking rationally, and abandon food, drink, friends, and life as they know it.

Mrs Batliwalla, Karl's maths teacher, thought differently. She felt exams were necessary as they empowered the teacher. All year long the children got the better of the establishment, but exams turned these cocky juveniles into whimpering stubs. Mrs Batliwalla (whose name literally meant 'bottle person' or 'person of the bottle' or 'personable bottle'), for example, had been given various nicknames, such as 'Batlee', 'The Batlees', and even 'The Batlee Axe'. The jokes ranged from the obvious: 'Oh look Batlee's lost weight, she's a half litre now', to the ridiculous: 'If Bruce Lee and Batlee had kids, would their daughter be called Leelee?' Mrs Batliwalla particularly had it in for boys like Karl who never seemed to understand that rhetorical questions weren't meant to be answered.

'Mr Marshall, history has divided people into three categories—those who can count, those who you can count on, and those who don't count at all. To which category do you belong?'

Pat would come the reply, 'I'd like a fourth category please—those who voluntarily like to be counted out.'

Muffled laughter would follow. So teachers like Batliwalla waited it out, waited for examinations to return and turn the tide in their favour.

If Karl was no academic, Kunal was worse. Kunal's bête noir, besides vegetarian food, was science. As he astutely observed, science was a subject that didn't seem to have much confidence in itself. After all, only subjects that didn't have faith in themselves kept subdividing themselves into smaller subjects as did science, by conveniently shrinking itself into physics, chemistry, and biology, which in turn were subdivided into metaphysics, eminently forgotten physics, stuff to do with magnets, something where light plays a part, and finally one of the following—refraction, reflection, and relaxation.

Both boys were bitterly disillusioned by mathematics once they discovered that 'algorithm' was not a musical term. Algebra in particular was a bugbear. Once when Mrs Batlee asked Karl to answer an algebraic expression that began, 'If you had seventeen oranges...' Karl promptly interrupted her by saying he was allergic to oranges and could she repeat the question with his more favoured foods like cold cuts or hard-boiled eggs? Kunal was far worse. His days as a mathematician ended prematurely when he realized he didn't have any more fingers for counting.

The reason, dear reader, we are examining both these points is that just in case these two gentlemen are destined for greatness, as indeed they might be later in my account, it is worth emphasizing that their early days show surprisingly little potential for anything extraordinary. Which brings us to Chekhov's most famous quote: 'Greatness, like mascara, must be bought and applied at very affordable market prices.'

Living from day to day, and grappling with school, exams, girls, and telephones, neither Karl nor Kunal could see what lay beyond the immediate future. Childhood and adolescence were a blur of pornographic magazines, castles in the air, and imitations of Amitabh Bachchan. Life was lived for the moment, and difficult and mundane matters such as exams and girlfriends were dealt with without much forethought, and usually only at the very last minute.

chapter 3

Like the vast majority of 'ungreat' childhoods (and here I include Winston Churchill, Euripides, Caligula, and Queen Victoria), Karl and Kunal got through school, girls, and puberty unscathed. Now, let us turn to how the duo went on from school to college! A simple answer is that they took a bus, but the process of going to college in Mumbai is fraught with uncertainty; it involves much manpower, daylight saving time, and thousands of phone calls. Okay I lied, perhaps less than a few thousand, but keep in mind this was 1988, long long before Kantibehen Shah invented the mobile phone and then refused to share his knowledge.

I'm going to let you in on a secret now. It has to do with the application process that's used for gaining admission into Mumbai's more prestigious colleges. It's a complicated seventeen-step process in which your parents play an important role.

Step 1:   Your parents wake up and brush each other's teeth. (Bear in mind they may brush their own teeth instead, although in certain circles this practice is considered both medieval and outlandish.)

Step 2:   After ablutions and a light breakfast, they leave the house at precisely 4:47 in the morning.

Step 3: They separate into two groups.

Step 4: Group one heads to Prestigious College A, also known as St Xavier's. Group B heads to Prestigious College B, also known as HR (Hassaram Rijhumal).

Step 5: At their respective Prestigious Colleges, they stand at the back of the 9-kilometre-long line. It is now 5:11 in the morning.

Step 6: For the next seven hours, they stand expressionless in the line.

Step 7: At 3:34 in the afternoon, they reach a window, but are persuaded not to break the glass.

Step 8: At 5:29 pm, they get to the official who hands them the CEF (College Entrance Form). This form is priceless. To quantify its worth, it's twice the GDP of Canada in 1988.

Step 9: The form is filled and deposited in a box.

Step 10: It is now 6:00 pm, and the time is put to good use by distracting other parents from filling in competitive forms. This is done in a subtle, refined manner by pulling apart the cheeks and exposing at least three inches of tongue.

Step 11: Both groups return home and celebrate by berating their child for getting only a modest 67 per cent in the tenth standard board exam.

Step 12: Wake up at the same unearthly hour and repeat the process, only to find out if Junior has been shortlisted for the interview. He has.

Step 13: Start one-month-long coaching classes to prepare Junior for the interview. Preparatory questions vary from the difficult 'What is your name?' to the very difficult 'What is your father's name?' to the impossible 'What is your name, again?'

Step 14: Wake up at some godforsaken hour and ensure the child stands in line for his interview. This is done by forming a chain of command. This is also known as a sandwich. This formation has Mom in front, Junior in the middle, and Dad in the rear. This is done to ensure three things: (a) Junior doesn't run away, (b) Junior doesn't sacrifice his turn to a pretty girl at the back of the line, and (c) if either parent has a heart attack, the other parent is still available to complete the mission.

Step 15: At the interview, Junior responds to all questions with his name or his father's name. This causes trouble when it comes to question seven, which is, 'Who formulated the constitution of India? And how many coffee breaks were taken during this formation?'

Step 16: Ten days later, or Monday, the family stands in line again, only to check on a board whether Junior's number has been accepted or not.

Step 17: Number 119 is accepted. Great news! Sadly, 119 isn't Junior's number. Finally they see that 127 has been accepted, and the family decides to go with this whether it's Junior's number or not. Wild celebrations break out, normally performed six inches away from the noses of those kids who didn't make it.

And so Karl and Kunal entered college. Let's pause and reflect for a second here, not just because this is a momentous occasion but more importantly because I need to pee.

Yes, we really should start the book from here as everything that happened before was essentially a waste of time. Indeed, dear reader, college is where a book really should begin. College onwards, a person's life becomes very interesting indeed. There are two reasons for this—he now enters an age where he has long pants, and also sex, and sometimes both together.

Karl and Kunal both got admission into Mumbai's foremost bastion of liberal thought (evidenced by the fact that boys were allowed to wear both shorts and lipstick)—St Xavier's College. Sadly, the loves of their lives thus far, Serena and Priya, didn't make it to the same institution, which was probably a good thing as it meant no more distractions. The boys could now concentrate on more varied experiences, namely, other girls.

St Xavier's had all the things a Mumbai college should have, three walls painted vaguely in the same colour, lots of youngsters, a stern watchman, a sherbatwala, a sandwichwala, no parking, and two guard dogs. It also offered education. Sorry not just education, but...er...space. Space was, is, and probably will be at a premium in Mumbai. This is unlike America where space is seen as the final frontier. St Xavier's College is one of those select few colleges (they can be counted on one finger of one hand), which actually had some space on its campus. This caused a huge problem with sexually starved, biting-at-the-reins sixteen-year-old boys, as you could spend the whole day at the college without actually touching anyone.

On the first day that they entered college, Karl and Kunal saw something that renewed their faith in God. Before them in the foyer, they counted 124 new students. Precisely 124 freshers or, to give them their Latin name, first year junior college students (FYJCS). Out of that crowd of 124, Karl counted 87 girls and just 37 boys. Their chances of making it just doubled, and miraculously they had only just stepped about two and a half feet into the college. What a place. No wonder the place was named after a saint; they couldn't have been more than a few steps from heaven, or—as they later discovered her name to be—from Tisha.

But just as the two boys were beginning to experience paradise on earth, they bumped into the first subject on the syllabus, ragging. Karl had never ever expected to meet a man called Schubert. Nobody is actually supposed to meet a man called Schubert. After the great composer died, his name has rarely been used. Occasionally, it has surfaced on the odd Rottweiler or domesticated hamster. Yet on day one, in that beautiful college with its bountiful female population (perhaps a case of too much advertising), Karl literally bumped into Schubert. Now Schubert stood 6 feet 3 inches and was 86 per cent light pole, 14 per cent water. He also had on his head something that at first the boys mistook for a Ridley turtle, then realized was a boa constrictor, only to be told that it was really a cap. Schubert was in pursuit of excellence, not so much in the academic field but in that of ragging. Ragging of course is one of India's four national sports, along with staining, spitting, and violating personal space. Schubert was too quick to show his deftness at all four sports. Along with two or three of his cronies, he identified four or five potential victims.

Karl and Kunal would have escaped attention except for Karl involuntarily doing a 'Xaverian'. A Xaverian is a peculiar phenomenon exhibited only by male animals on the St Xavier's campus. It refers to a strange, oft-repeated process wherein a male's head follows a pretty young thing even while the rest of his body walks away in a different direction. Thus, as Karl followed the ravishing Tisha, his chest rammed straight into Schubert's knee. It was a no contest; the beanpole—also known as the ragger-in-charge—collapsed on to the floor. Kunal saw what was coming next, but even as he tried to shout a warning, he realized it was too late. Being a true friend and loyal supporter, and someone who always had Karl's back, he did the next best thing and fled.

Karl and the other victims were lined up against a wall. First, he was asked to repeat a few words by way of formal introduction. They highlighted three points: (1) Karl was a practising homosexual, (2) Karl enjoyed drinking his own pee, (3) Karl would serve Schubert lunch for the next 39 years.

Karl was then asked to state what he was good at. Karl's tongue, which had gone into a state of panic and wasn't cooperating with his brain, said incredibly, 'Swimming'. Soon, a water bottle was found, its contents emptied on the floor. Karl was then asked to strip to his underwear and swim in roughly 250 ml of water. Karl's tongue tripped again. The words, 'Kunal... help', came out in a gasp. Kunal who was cowering 130 feet away was identified and brought forward.

As the two boys lay on their backs, demonstrating India's first synchronized swimming movements, Karl couldn't help thinking that they were not off to a very good start. However, one good thing did come of it—all 87 girls had seen them naked. In fact, all 87 girls were aware of three things—who they were, that they liked to swim, and that they both wore the same brand of underwear. A standing ovation greeted the end of the swim. Of course, Schubert also insisted that they pretend to towel each other off before slipping on their clothes. How Karl wished Schubert was in reality a hamster.

Now you know how sometimes when you feel everything is crumbling around you, suddenly something wonderful happens? Well, as Karl was putting on his T-shirt, Tisha said, 'Hello.' The power of that single word energized Karl with 10,000 volts of electricity. Okay I'm exaggerating, it was actually more like 9,000 volts. In his head, he had already climbed halfway up the tallest mountain, having just swum the deepest river, without using his hands.

First impressions are very important for the opposite sex. That's one of the main reasons Michael Jackson never made much headway with the ladies. As Karl prepared his reply to the most mouth-watering hello he'd ever heard, his brain went through all the possible replies at high speed. He had to quickly choose between 'Hello! How are you?', 'Wozz up', 'Hi, I'm Karl', and 'Ding dong bell'. He came up with 'The underwears are both mine; this Kunal is always flicking my things.'

Here, Karl was setting a very important precedent. A precedent that continues throughout this book and its three sequels: when in doubt, when unsure, blame Kunal. Tisha who had by now realized she could have a much better conversation with a salamander, smiled quizzically and walked out of sight. Karl would have tried to explain himself to her, but he found that he couldn't breathe. This was probably because Schubert and two of his cronies were hugging him round the waist. Apparently he had passed his initiation with flying colours and had been 'accepted'. He tried to break the good news to Kunal, but Kunal was nowhere to be seen. In fact, he was buried under the weight of eight senior students who were in the process of conveying to him the good news that he'd been 'accepted' as well, but couldn't miss out on the opportunity to aim a few boots at Kunal's well-padded torso.

Having extricated themselves, the two boys quickly regained their composure; after all, they now had the seniors' blessings. They both broke into rather cocky walks. Karl walked as if he was carrying a large fish tank between his legs, Kunal as if he was carrying the fish itself.

The first period (I hate that word, and by the way, where are the feminists now?) was a high-pressure affair. The first five minutes in a new class can set up the dynamic for the rest of the year. Karl and Kunal chose the second last row of the class. They needn't have bothered. The class was huge, and it offered ample opportunity to go unnoticed by the teacher, which of course is the sole aim of every self-respecting student who ever went to college. The first class was economics; the teacher Mrs Pherwani wore a saree that had ceased to fit her ages ago. As Mrs Pherwani plunged into the 64 Marshall laws, Karl and Kunal started taking notes. They listened attentively to every word, and patiently compiled their research, which was a list of the twenty most attractive girls in the room. This was no easy job.

College was very different from school. Firstly, college was taller. Then there was the small matter of homework. Here, the definition changed to work that could be left at home. The boys realized quite early that to get through college all they really had to do was turn up, and with a roughly 80 per cent female population, turn up they did.

Did you think youngsters enter college to sharpen their minds by acquiring an education? Wrong! Youngsters enter college to sharpen their minds at the ancient Roman art of filibustering. Karl figured that in the more flexible environment of college, it was far easier to engage a teacher in a time-consuming, long-drawn-out dialogue. A normal exchange between Karl and a teacher would go like this:

Teacher: Is anyone familiar with the works of the war poet Wilfred Owen?

Karl: Yes, Ma'am, but I'm more fascinated by one of the poets who influenced him, the Moroccan playwright and amateur wrestler Abu Bin Saeed, who was the first African one-legged writer of prose to be accepted by Western intellectuals, if I may recite one of his most famous verses from the poem 'The Road that Runs to Ruins'?

Teacher: Go on.

Karl: Don't chew on his camel's fat Fatima,
His life isn't worth the dung.
Oft this repeated falsely Fatima,
His palace is notably strung,
The ancient ashes berate a secret untold,
Shared by the lust of the past,
A Naked Falcon rambles, his wings unfurled
Haunted by his melodious grasp.

Not wanting to appear unschooled and having no authoritative point of reference like Google to turn to in those days, the teacher would play it safe by allowing a slight digression from Wilfred Owen to the non-existent Abu Bin Saeed. This episode is important in the context of what Karl wanted to do with his life, a dream that could be summed up in the single phrase 'not much'. Also, he was clearly honing a particular skill, one that would later become his life's work—that of a professional 'fabricator' dedicated to the public good.

Colleges in urban India are very different from the schools. While schools try to exercise control and and impose a disciplined regimen, colleges offer a great deal of flexibility and choice. If you ask any college kid what he thinks the greatest thing about college is, the first four things he will mention will be (a) that you don't have to cut your hair, (b) the presence of girls, (c) that girls don't have to cut their hair, and (d) that there are no uniforms. Moreover, the biggest incentive behind going to college is the phenomenon of flexible timings. If the 7:55 am lecture was too early, you could avoid it and go straight to the 8:50 one. If 8:50 was still way too early, you could begin with the 9:40 one. And if that was far too early (and indeed it was), you could come in after the break. What most self-respecting freshers did was to sit in the canteen and wonder which lecture to attend, and invariably ended up doing the decent thing and attending none at all. Karl and Kunal were no different. They soon understood the centrality of the canteen to their higher education. Great debates and arguments were held at this darbar, and subjects ranged from who had the best legs to who was most likely to tie a rakhi on you.

It was during the first term that Karl fell in love for the first time. And I mean real deep love. This prompted him to perform an unparalleled act of bravery to win her fair hand. Great heroes in the past have composed beautiful concertos, invaded cities, or killed their own brothers for the love of a woman. Karl took this much further. He switched from Hindi to Russian.

Nisha was his polar opposite—quiet, dignified, private, and shy—but who can explain love? One

60

look at her comely figure in tight blue jeans and an oversized shirt and Karl went down like the *Titanic*.

A strange thing usually happened in her presence; Karl sensed something like a 200 per cent increase in energy. He also noticed that when Nisha was around, he'd bounce. He'd sort of jump up and down on the spot a lot. She merely had to pass by and he'd bounce. If he heard her voice, there would be a bounce, and if she was expected in the vicinity, he would find himself bouncing. Unfortunately, Nisha was not very communicative. You would not find her drinking milk off the floor to win a challenge, or burping the alphabet in public. Worse still, she was studying Russian, a subject you could choose instead of Hindi. The only problem was that it was the first lecture of the day. Now having just been released from prison, no college fresher was keen on the early morning lecture. Yet, Russian was Russian, and Nisha was Nisha, so Karl, in a supreme act of love, made the switch.

Karl soon realized that love didn't come easy in Russian. On his first lecture, he chose to sit in the back row, as far as possible from Nisha; after all, he didn't want to make his feelings too obvious.

Any romantic illusions he may have had were slapped out of him during the first lecture itself. Russian had to be the most difficult language in the world. It has approximately 3,571 letters of two types, both big and small. The big ones unfortunately have no connection with the small. They aren't in any way related, and neither do they share the same genes. So, in effect, you have to learn 7,142 different letters, all uniquely dissimilar from one another.

A quick mental calculation told him that learning this alphabet by heart might take him 47½ years. By which time Nisha would be 63 years old. Things were not going according to plan. But there was worse to come.

In Hindi, Karl would scrape by with 50 per cent, with great difficulty. In his first test in Russian, he got 4 out of 50, which is 8 per cent in Russian or any other language. Karl went into depression. Along with three other 'weak' students, he was called in for extra classes. Needless to say, Nisha was not among them.

Unfortunately, we need to wrap up the college story soon, because of the following unexpected reasons: (a) my publisher's deadlines, (b) the whole college epic would take too long, (c) I'm bored. But before we end it and finally begin the actual story, there are a couple of college anecdotes that need to be told. Let's begin with the tale of the elevator, commonly known by its Indian name, the lift. St Xavier's had a dark secret unknown to most except a few members of the staff and a boy called Kevin who had taken eleven years to clear the five-year course. Given the labyrinth of large staircases at St Xavier's, many students carrying heavy books and even heavier make-up were constantly plagued by injury. A trip from the canteen to the third floor was genuinely so risky that even teachers would start the day early to be on the safer side. But somewhere near the canteen was a secret door which led to one of modern man's three greatest inventions—the lift. Yes, the lift along with the air-conditioner and eyeliner are the three discoveries that separate us from animals. Let's accept it, no one has ever seen a chimpanzee wearing eyeliner and operating an air-conditioned lift, have they?

The lift had a caretaker whose name was Prabhu. The lift was used only by teachers and peons. However, due to a slight accident of nature (Prabhu had a severe case of halitosis), most would rather risk injury rather than encounter Prabhu in a claustrophobic little iron box. Indifferent to class prejudices, Karl and Kunal decided to befriend Prabhu. They did this by offering him their faded old shirts as presents. They would take an old shirt, have it washed and pressed, then packed in a newish-looking plastic bag, after which they'd hand it over to an excited Prabhu. Sometimes, for good measure, they even splashed a bit of cologne on the shirt. But in a matter of seconds, the cologne lost the battle against Prabhu's own overpowering scent. In this professional exchange of old used goods for services, Karl and Kunal gradually gained control of the lift.

Initially, they were forced to stomach Prabhu's presence, but over time, they convinced him to stand as sentry outside the lift to watch out for any stray, unwanted members of the teaching staff. This was a foolproof plan, because the moment a staff member—in fact the moment any living organism— saw Prabhu, they'd rush away. Prabhu could thus be regarded as an evolved scarecrow, used simply to scare away teachers.

Control of the lift meant more power for Karl and Kunal. They started offering lift rides to curry favours, and the scheme became very popular among teachers too. Even the odd teacher who had successfully

63

circumvented Prabhu pleaded innocently for a chance to hitch a ride. And soon, girls, boys, teachers, and peons all depended on Karl and Kunal for a safer mode of travel.

The other incident we feel obliged to review is the curious case of the prom. After the failure of the 'Russian revolution', Nisha and Karl actually became friends. By using the famous 'reverse pyramid technique', they might even have regarded each other as 'good' friends. The reverse pyramid technique can be traced to Pharaoh Ahflután, the Sixth. Ahflutan who was notably fond of his drink came up with the idea of rebuilding a few pyramids using an opposite technique. He insisted on the smallest and weakest slab of stone being used for the base of the pyramid, after which the slabs would get larger and stronger in keeping with the principle of the ascending order. It must be noted that many Third World governments follow the same system quite successfully.

By the time the fifth brick was laid, the whole pyramid would come crashing down, but Ahflutan persisted with this approach. It was only after 5 million labourers had been crushed (seventeen of them to death), that the Pharaoh put an end to the ridiculous practice, and began to build sea-facing bungalows with built-in swimming pools and infra-red heating technology instead. The Four Seasons, still run by the Pharaoh's family, offers these deluxe facilities.

For Karl, the reverse pyramid meant they'd start out as the two of them, and then more and more friends would be added to make Nisha feel more comfortable. For example, if Nisha and Karl began with an unnecessary conversation on say flossing, within no time others would join and fatten the group. Thus, a weak slab was strengthened by subsequent layers, and Nisha eventually found herself quite comfortable with Karl and his...er...pyramid.

Karl decided to try his luck at the upcoming prom. At its largest, Karl's group in college numbered over a hundred. Since about 30 per cent of this group was from the science stream, a whole lot of experiments were conducted, most of them involving glasses, lime slices, and large quantities of alcohol. Every weekend, there was a party held to celebrate important events like Ashish's new haircut or Sadia's blue blouse or Nimish's additions to his CD collection. The parties were held at any location that didn't have parents present on the premises. The scientists could then continue with their experiments in peace and unquiet.

It was during one of these parties that Kunal reminded Karl about the prom, which was scheduled for two weekends later. Karl after mustering up all his courage decided to take matters into his own hands. The initial conversation flowed something like this, although a word or two may have gotten misplaced on account of the awful sound (that some philistines mistook for music) blaring in the background.

Karl: Great party, huh?

Nisha: Yes.

Karl: Er...great party, huh?

Nisha: Yeh. I think so.

Karl: Great party, huh...

Nisha: Er, can you pass the chips?

Karl: Great party, huh?

Karl thought to himself, 'That went swimmingly.' He had made some early inroads for the prom conversation, which he could now approach in round two.

Karl: Would you like some chips?

Nisha: Oh, thanks.

Karl: Great party, huh?

Nisha: Yup.

Karl: Would you like some chips?

Nisha: Thanks.

The woman was clearly all over him. Literally and figuratively eating out of his hand, Karl thought to himself. Yup, round two had gone swimmingly too. Now it was time to administer the coup de grâce in round three.

Karl: Chips!

Nisha: No, thanks.

Karl: Great party.

Nisha: I know, great party.

Karl: Er…chips.

Nisha: No, but it's getting late, my deadline's 11:30 pm. Do you mind walking me home?

Karl nearly had a heart attack. In junior college, a girl asking to be walked home is roughly equivalent to an adult woman asking you to marry her. Round three clearly belonged to him. He composed himself by pulling at his belt buckle twice and braced himself for round four, where the coup de grâce would now have to be administered.

'No problem, let's go,' he said.

It was dark outside. As round four wound down, he decided to go in for the kill.

Karl: Great party, huh.

Nisha: Karl, if you mention the party again, I swear…

Karl: Okay, okay, we better talk softly, people are sleeping.

During the ten-minute walk down the road, they broke into a more fluid conversation. Nisha discussed her parents' wrath, especially her mother's raw anger when she missed her deadlines. She couldn't help wondering aloud why Karl was sweating despite the nip in the night air. As the conversation turned to her favourite actor, Patrick Swayze, Karl shared his secret with her. Patrick Swayze was his favourite actor too. He also made a mental note to find out who exactly Patrick Swayze was and perhaps learn the names of at least five of his films, especially the one-word ones if any.

As they reached her building compound, Karl realized that it was now or never. As she opened the lift door and entered, he mustered up all his courage and finally said, 'Great par…' Nisha immediately cautioned him, 'Karl I…anyway, thanks for walking me home. I'll see you in class tomorrow. Good night.' With that, she pressed the lift button.

It was then that Karl experienced a life-defining moment. When his eyeballs were directly in line with her feet, Karl shouted, 'Nisha, one second please?' Nisha stopped the lift, and looked out at him. 'Would you like to go with me to the prom?' Karl squealed at her shoes. The shoes seemed to nod their approval. 'Great,' Karl exhaled. He couldn't help recording how beautiful her knee looked that night. 'But Karl, it's not a date, right?' Nisha asked. Karl staggered. 'Of course not, it's not a date. A date would mean only two people; we have hundreds of people with us, there's Irfan, Kunal, Parag, Sweety, Samir, Vikram, Sumeet, Vishal, Imran, Kaushik, Tanvi, Shalini, Renu, Smita...' But by then, Nisha's shoes had stopped communicating and Nisha had vanished.

Karl went home like a headless chicken. Part of him was very excited that he had tasted success, but part of him was a little worried that he'd have to go to great pains to prove the upcoming prom night wasn't really a date. Pains such as repeating 'It's not a date' 247 consecutive times throughout the evening. As an afterthought, he shelved the plan. He had many bridges to cross first: (a) learn how to shave, (b) find a suit, (c) ensure that Irfan, Kunal, Parag, Sweety, Samir, Vikram, Sumeet, Vishal, Imran, Kaushik, Tanvi, Shalini, Renu, and Smita all agreed to be part of Team Karl on prom night. In the days leading to the night, Karl made it a point to play it a little cool. Besides, he avoided talking on core topics like the prom, parties, and dates. However, his constant and sudden love for Patrick Swayze did appear a little misplaced.

By the time prom night arrived, he had altered his father's suit, which was originally blue, but had over the course of 27 years become a rather dirty black. He also trimmed his whiskers for the first time. He thus came to hold the dubious record of being the second last male in his class to shave, with Vinay Agrawal being the last. Of course, three or four girls also made that list. Shaving was one of the most overrated chores Karl had ever known. Only clipping toenails could have been more dreary. His geyser would fog the mirror in 34 seconds, and hence, Karl learnt to live by a golden rule—shave whatever you can in 34 seconds. The rest can stay.

On the night itself, Kunal directed the taxi to Karl's house, and then they picked up Kunal's date, Prema. Equipped with a buffer, they went all the way back to Nisha's house. As an added measure, Karl sent Kunal up to escort her to the cab.

Nisha looked stunning in a green chiffon outfit, which Kunal felt could have been anything from a shirt to a tent, and was in fact, the result of a union between the two. As Kunal occupied the front seat, Nisha squirmed into the back, jamming Karl between the two ladies. That made Karl squirm with fear, and he unwittingly pushed against Prema hard enough for her to object loudly. But Karl didn't seem particularly apologetic. He certainly wasn't going to move in the opposite direction lest he came into contact with Nisha. Physical contact would mean he thought it was a date. By the time they reached the brightly lit college, Karl was virtually perched on a hapless Prema's lap.

A society's sense of civilization is defined by: (a) how it treats its animals, (b) how it controls poverty and disease, and (c) whether booze is allowed. In that sense, St Xavier's College was found wanting. True, animals didn't necessarily get a bad deal at the college, a couple even graduated now and then, but booze on campus was a strict no-no. As with booze bans worldwide, this led only to one thing—even more booze being consumed. The trick was in the clothes. In fact, suits were designed by Alfred P Suit, an American tailor living in prohibition-bound Chicago, to outwit the booze restrictions. As the restrictions grew more stringent, he took to designing large suits with even larger pockets; and each pocket was designed with a single intent and purpose—to stash small quantities of booze.

Karl and Kunal were not yet heavy drinkers, but both felt that this was one occasion on which a nip or two wouldn't hurt. This meant that when the slow dances began, Karl readily abandoned Rule 48 of the date, which was exactly the same as Rules 1–47, i.e. 'You will not dance with your partner'. Alcohol had made him rather bold and reckless. He almost commanded Nisha to dance in a way Errol Flynn would have been proud of, and as he held her shapely hips, Karl could hear cash registers ringing away. (He was told later that there had been a drum solo in the middle of the slow dance, but he hadn't been listening very carefully at the time.)

As the song ended, Karl asked, 'Are you having fun?'
Nisha: Yes, but for one thing.
Karl: What?
Nisha: Can you please get off my foot?
Karl: Oh...er...Great party.
Nisha: I suppose you'll be offering me chips next?
But as she smiled indulgently when she spoke, Karl knew he had touched a chord, or at least a hip, a most tempting hip. Thus began Karl Marshall's first serious romance.

chapter 4

One lazy afternoon, while the class savoured that sense of idle pleasure possible only in a teacher's absence, a young lady entered their space with a large white piece of paper, which she promptly tacked to the bulletin board. This aroused the boys' curiosity, and they began grading the lady immediately. Piyush gave her an 8 on 10 for her figure, and Vikram was toying with the idea of a 7; but it was Karl who actually read the notice's headline while drinking in her sophisticated manner. 'Actors wanted.' The note was unambiguous. 'Actors, singers, dancers wanted for a new musical called *Godspell*.' The boys chose to ignore the notice, but what they couldn't ignore was what was happening *around* the notice. Around 50 of the college's most nubile, sexy, and striking females had gathered near the board, showing great interest in the sheet of paper. Gazing upon that bevy of beauties, the boys instinctively understood the truth of the proverb, 'If you wanna score with the chicks, join theatre.' Chaucer, Shakespeare, and Strindberg had based their choice of a career on this philosophy. Karl and Kunal quickly noted the address and time for the audition. 'JB Petit School, 5 to 7 this evening.' Today's afternoon siesta needed to be cut short.

As the two boys knocked on the rear door of the school's assembly hall, it opened magically by itself. A booming voice enquired who they were and what they wanted, using the universal word that expresses all queries, 'Yes?' Completely spooked by the magic door, the two boys walked around looking for the source of the voice. 'Yes?' The boom was even more emphatic now, but they could find no trace yet of where the voice was coming from. 'Morons, I'm here,' said a commanding voice. There, right in front of them, a little over five feet tall, stood the Queen of Mumbai's theatre scene, Pearl Padamsee. The boys had never seen anything like this. A person with a voice three times her size.

'Go stand in the back of the line. What are your names? Doesn't matter for now, you'll be A and you'll be B. Moron A and Moron B.'

Kunal couldn't help feeling a little downcast that he'd been assigned the 'B' status. Over 30 people waited in line to be auditioned. Thankfully, most were girls. The bad news, however, was that the boys were immediately surrounded by other males. The audition process was particularly severe. A middle-aged man, another young woman, and Pearl sat behind a huge desk. Then they'd call out a name. The person would sing, dance, or act out a passage from a script handed to them. After they finished, the three judges would look blankly at the performer and simply say, 'Next'.

A normal conversation went something like this:
Pearl: Name?
Tapan: Tapan Joshi.

Pearl: Age?

Tapan: 17.

Pearl: What would you like to do?

Tapan: Sing. I've got this song called Wond...

Pearl: Okay, dance.

Tapan: Actually I'm a singer.

Pearl: Just dance.

Tapan: But I can't dance, I'm actually a singer, I'd like to do...

Pearl: Dance, you have 90 seconds.

Tapan: I'm not really a dancer, I'm...

Pearl: Next.

Kunal began to sweat. He always panicked a good half hour before anyone else, and sensing the general fear in the room, Kunal sweated buckets. But it was too late. As the great Caesar once said, the die had been cast.

Pearl: Name?

Kunal: Kunal...er...

Pearl: Aha, Moron A!

Kunal: No, actually I'm Moron B, he's Moron A.

Pearl: What would you like to do?

Kunal: Well, I'd like to go to the bathroom.

Pearl: That's your talent? You really are a moron.

Kunal: No, it's just that we drank two glasses of sugarcane juice.

Pearl: We are not interested, repeat, not interested. Now, do you act, sing, or dance?

Kunal: See like that I'm not good at singing or dancing, but I'd really appreciate it if you let Karl, I mean, Moron A, up first while I go to the bathroom.

Pearl: Turn to page 71 in the script in front of you

73

and read out the monologue from the top of the page. You're Harry.

Kunal: No, no, I'm Kunal, there must be some mistake.

Pearl: Read!

Kunal froze in fear. All eyes were on him. Kunal read as only he could, like a blind elephant thrashing through an obstacle course. We've all heard people like Kunal. They like to read one word, then pause, then read the next, then stumble, then read another word, then pause. There was a ripple of laughter in the room.

One of the other judges stopped Kunal with his head.

Judge 2: I like his interpretation, Harry as a retard? Nicely done.

Judge 3: Yes, a slow Harry, it could work.

Pearl: Leave your name and contact number with Diane, Moron B.

Kunal: Can I please go to the toilet?

And thus destiny conspired to trap Kunal, much against his wishes, in the clutches of theatre. Karl suffered an even worse fate.

Pearl: Name?

Karl: Karl, Moron...

Pearl: Not interested, repeat, not interested. Now, do you sing, act, or dance?

Karl: Act, I've taken part in three school... er, plays.

Pearl: Same as before. Not interested, repeat, not interested. Okay, sing, go ahead.

Karl: Actually I'd prefer to read out a passage from the script?

Pearl: Not interested, repeat, not interested. Now I'm counting to four and you had better have started singing. One, two, three, four.

As she completed her countdown, Karl decided to let her have it. He belted out 'Santa Lucia' just as he had heard Mario Lanza and Beniamino Gigli sing it all his life. After he finished, with an unnecessary dramatic flourish and holding the note, he knew they were impressed.

Judge 2: But can you sing anything in English?

Karl: Look, I told you I'd prefer to act, but Ma'am forced me to sing and…

Pearl: Moron A, not interested, repeat, not interested. Fortunately for you your singing is much better than your conversation. Give your particulars to Diane, and ah one more thing.

Karl: Yes.

Pearl: Get out.

Karl and Kunal stopped to catch their breath outside the school. They had come here to meet girls, and now they had been chosen for a musical over many others, a musical they couldn't care less about. They had mixed feelings about Mumbai theatre's overlord. While Karl felt Pearl was putting on a hard act and was actually quite charming, Kunal was convinced that she would physically hurt him if she could; besides what kind of adult stops another from going to the toilet?

The rehearsals for *Godspell* were to be held at JB Petit School itself. The play, which is set to music, loosely traces the life of Christ. The main lead was a young man who went by the name of Bugs. Bugs, though extremely gifted, had another peculiarity—he was really fat. A fat Jesus!

On day one, Pearl gathered all the actors around. They totalled thirteen. Karl was pleased that six of them were girls, thank God for theatre. Always the pessimist, Kunal was quick to note that five were boys.

Pearl: Okay, introduce yourselves to one another, and follow my four simple rules.

One. The whistle around my neck is your supreme commander. When it blows, you stop everything and freeze. If you are crossing the road and you hear it, you stop and freeze even though there may be a truck coming right at you at 90 miles per hour.

Karl: Ma'am, trucks in Mumbai aren't equipped to go at that speed…

There was some muffled laughter, but surprisingly, Pearl didn't caution the speaker.

Pearl: Moron A, if Moron B gets hit by the truck, it's the truck we'll have to worry about.

More laughter. Kunal put on his 'What did I do' expression.

Pearl: Two. You will not bunk rehearsal. Especially on flimsy grounds like a death in the family, being terminally ill, or communal riots in your lane.

Three. You will carry your own bottle of water and not make demands on our crew.

Four. You will not bring friends to rehearsal, whether they are sons, daughters, lovers, or all of the above. No companions hanging around.

Karl: I've already flouted rule four then. I've brought my good friend, Moron B here. Shall I ask him to wait outside?

More laughter.

Pearl: In his case we'll make an exception. Looking the way he does, he's lucky to have a friend.

More laughter. Kunal for his part had perfected the 'What did I do' expression, the look of the poor, pale, gaunt, hapless, persecuted victim. Well, about as poor, pale, gaunt, and hapless as a 92 kilo, 5 foot 6 inch teenager can appear at any rate. That became his signature look—a look that both came to be identified with him and defined him.

Our two heroes actually started enjoying theatre. Initially a hard taskmaster, no make that taskmistress, Pearl turned out to have a somewhat caustic sense of humour. Kunal and a girl called Zenobia became her favourite whipping boys, so to speak. The large cast of *Godspell* plus the backstage crew easily totalled over twenty on any given day. Little did they know that this would be twice the number of members in the audience for *Godspell* on any given night.

During this phase, Kunal experienced a period of growth from the waist up. He had what is in today's parlance called an Indian Male Physique, characterized by matchstick legs, a large waist, heavy torso, thick neck, and jaws that might have sent a pitbull terrier into early heat. In the West, this is known as the 'lollipop figure'. As his weak legs started carrying a skyscraper, Kunal started walking with a stagger, much like a drunk sailor. Kunal had another remarkable habit—he wore what Pearl called Christian 'condom' shorts. These shorts started at the waist and, well, ended there too. They were less than three inches in length, which led to certain obvious jokes about their contents.

Sample I:

Q: What's Kunal got in his shorts?

A: Nothing.

Sample II:

Q: What's the similarity between Kunal's shorts and the Union Budget?

A: They both deliver nothing.

Sample III:

Q: What's the similarity between Kunal's shorts and an Anaconda?

A: Nothing.

Further, Kunal would stuff his ample torso (which was easily the size of Barbados) into the shorts' waistband; note that the waistband was itself half the length of the shorts. This particular practice gave him the appearance of an inflated balloon, and led one to expect a jolly nature of him, even though he was going through his persecuted victim phase. A torso shoved into a pair of shorts coupled with a 'What did I do' lent him a particularly striking appearance. It also made him easy meat, and I must emphasize that there was plenty of 'meat' there for Pearl, Karl, and the rest to have a few laughs at his expense.

Zenobia's was a different story. She was a girl with a beautiful voice. Unfortunately, the voice, like Pearl's, didn't fit her body. Zenobia had to have been the smallest person ever made. She stood an inch taller than a doll, with even smaller and softer features. She was the kind of lady who'd still be asked for identification in a bar at the age of 43. Zenobia only came alive when she was singing. Otherwise, her demure, quiet, almost apologetic ways often led her to be mistaken for very small furniture, like a weaned-out camel's saddle. Being so small for so long inevitably meant being the butt of a lot of jokes. A particularly common one was 'Zenobia, stand up,' to which her reply was always the obvious, 'But I am standing.'

Zenobia's passive demeanour made any caustic comments directed at her appear more cruel than usual. From Zenobia, there was never any repartee, no standing (oops) of her ground, if you'll excuse the insensitive phrasing. Yet, such a personality meant that Kunal and she had much in common. Hence, while the whippings continued unabated from all and sundry—Karl, Pearl, and Bugs, not to mention Delna, Lanza, Baba, and Darius—Kunal and Zenobia started developing a certain fondness for one another. Karl found himself feeling just a bit insecure about his devoted friend, who had begun splitting his loyalties. But Kunal wasn't the only person developing new relationships within the theatre circle.

As a general rule, a theatre group comprises actors, backstage people, the light and sound crew, and a director. Of course, if you are lucky, occasionally there's an audience as well. *Godspell* wasn't that lucky, but from no want of effort from all those involved. There were many different types of rehearsals. From 5 to 6 pm was the dance rehearsal, 6 to 7 pm was the singing rehearsal, 7 pm onwards was the real rehearsal, which simply meant that the first rehearsal was just a rehearsal for the second rehearsal, which in turn was a dress rehearsal for the real rehearsal.

Dance, for Karl, was an inhuman practice. He tried explaining the actual futility of dance to the choreographer, and how it is not practised in any evolved society without the dancer first imbibing large quantities of alcohol, a larger portion of which must also be administered to the audience. When this request was turned down, Karl decided to turn to his strongest talent—his ability to tell a lie. As Karl saw it, humans were the only animals who danced. No other animal suffered this indignity in public. I mean, can you imagine a lion and his wife doing a foxtrot, while a wild boar and an antelope laugh themselves silly at the sight? Animals look upon dancing as very unbecoming behaviour. Why then must humans make such fools of themselves? Try dancing in front of a few animals and watch their reactions. But since there didn't seem to be any way around dancing for the play, Karl decided to bring in the heavy artillery. He had done his research and read somewhere that hamstring injuries are the most recurrent. In the middle of a poorly executed routine, he grabbed his front leg and gasped aloud in a way that would have done a flamingo proud.

Choreographer: What is it?

Karl: I think I've torn my hamstring again.

He subtly threw in the 'again' to imply a certain athleticism, making himself sound like the kind of professional athlete who would readily push his body to its limits in an effort to break new ground.

Choreographer: The hamstring's in the back of your thigh, why are you holding the front?

Karl: Oh, my hamstrings always hurt in the front.

Judging from the laughter that filled the room, Karl realized that his knowledge of the human thigh wasn't particularly impressive. The derision that followed quietly replaced the hamstring.

It was while impersonating a human wallflower, with one leg cocked back, one hand thrown up, and his head hanging to the left, that Karl first espied the comely shape of Pia. To help salvage some semblance of masculinity, he tried immediately to unlock his leg, but gravity defeated him and he collapsed to the floor. Pia was turning blue trying not to laugh at him, but the dam soon burst. Karl regained his composure rapidly, and for the rest of the rehearsal, he danced terribly, but with élan nonetheless, like many Bollywood legends of yore. You can be out of sync for an entire dance, but if you end with a flourish (normally an expansive hand gesture moving around the head), all is forgiven.

Karl was the king of flourish. Truth be told, he practically invented flourish. But in an effort to impress a prospective mate, he went an extra mile with a twirl of the hand, returned for an encore, and then like a human windmill gone mad, performed about 77 more flourishes. Had he ended on number 44, he might have been all right, but the music had stopped long before he did, indeed all movement had stopped, and everyone watched his solo performance reach its climax.

Kunal led the mock applause. Comments followed thick and fast. 'The young Michael Jackson.' 'He should do a solo dance recital.' 'Obviously a trained Odissi dancer.' 'Available for private party celebrations and corporate functions.'

Karl made a mental note to cancel all flourishes in the future, and also decided this was not the right time to try and make an impression on Pia. He was stunned when a polite voice said, 'That was very... er, different. I'd only watch the play for you.' It was Pia. In a moment, Karl was hooked, booked, quartered, and served on a spit.

Pia was ravishing. Earlier that morning, Karl had just read a poem called 'Carpe Diem', which translates as 'seize the day'. Karl decided to ask Pia out that very day, his exact words being, 'Can I borrow your hairclip?' There was nothing unusual about this request as, like most boys in college, he had let his hair grow long, but it was difficult for Pia to ascertain the latent implication of a date. One can only be so subtle.

This was when fate played her hand. Okay, okay, it is rather ambiguous whether fate is a 'he' or a 'she', but it is commonly accepted that if anything is as mysterious and inexplicable as fate truly is, then it must be female, though there are exceptions to this rule, like the Bangladeshi cricket team and the late Michael Jackson. It was Bugs (who had been cast in the role of Jesus) who intervened and suggested that everyone join him for tender coconut water. Bugs was pure dynamite as an actor, and was wonderfully dynamic as a person. At an even 6 feet and 300 pounds, no one could have been more inappropriately named. There was nothing remotely bug-like about him. And he responded to most occasions and situations with 'Let's have some tender coconut water.'

This time, however, Karl was delighted to hear Bugs's oft-repeated suggestion. Soon, they were on their first date. The...er...three of them—Pia and Karl on either side, Bugs bang in the middle, going on and on about how to drink a tender coconut, at what angle to tip one's head, in how many sips to finish one's drink, how to croon to one's tender coconut... nurture a relationship, form a bond with it, etc. No man has done as much for tender coconut as Bugs. If he'd had his way, he may well have had a couple of actors on stage replaced by a couple of tender coconuts instead.

Bugs showered Karl with his attention, and filled up the void in his life. Bugs did this in three ways: (a) by chaperoning Karl around in his car, (b) by paying all his bills, and (c) by mistaking Karl for a tender coconut from time to time. Soon, a sort of bond grew between the three youngsters. Since Pia wasn't needed for all rehearsals, the two boys would go and fetch her in Bugs's vehicle, which could not be called a car by any leap of the imagination. An undefined shade of red, it may once have resembled a Maruti Omni but after countless cross-country trips, collisions, and modifications it looked more like the large shell of a huge dying hybrid of an insect and a marsupial. The shell had been christened 'Pratibha' by Bugs after his first girlfriend who was actually larger and slower. It was at this time, still well underage, that Karl started driving. Alright, it was more a holding of the steering wheel while still in the passenger seat for fifteen seconds whilst Bug lit up a smoke. It never proved dangerous, because in those fifteen seconds Pratibha moved exactly four and a half metres, so no damage could ever really be done. Bugs also introduced Karl to a unique honking technique—one long bleep followed immediately by a shorter, sharper one—a strategy Mozart used in one of his clarinet concertos.

After Pia joined them, they would leave for their eating orgy. Their two most favoured places were the famous Bade Miya and Kobe. Bade Miya was the work of a marketing genius. A takeaway stall had been set up on five feet of a public pavement, was run only in the evenings, with no overheads, and its proprietor laughed all the way to the bank, which incidentally was on the other pavement and often ordered from Bade Miya. The meat was usually quite old, the chutney older, and the cutlery had recently been traced to the Kushan dynasty under Kanishka the First who, legend has it, never wanted it back. Yet, the place was always packed with people lolling in their Pratibhas, eating baida rolls and boti kebabs and paneer tikka, which tasted and looked exactly the same. The three thespians would park Pratibha as far away from the crowded stall as possible, then (excuse the phrase) blow Pratibha till help arrived. Pia liked the boti kebab, Karl the chicken tangdi, and Bugs liked pretty much anything and everything. Then Bugs would make the payment and promptly force everyone into a round of tender coconut.

Let's face it, Pratibha was no Ferrari. However, Bugs's driving was the stuff of legend. It is said, in the 1980s, visitors from outside Mumbai would come to see three things—the Hanging Gardens (where if you spend close to three months you may find a garden), the Gateway of India, and Bugs driving his van. Till today, there is absolutely no evidence that Bugs actually made contact with the accelerator. In the event that Pratibha actually moved, most likely it was the wind's doing, or more specifically the sea breeze's, which was readily available in most parts of Mumbai. Casual walkers, stray dogs, senior citizens, and the odd paraplegic would all pass Pratibha by.

Bugs could also lay claim to another remarkable attribute. He would always, always catch the red light. Even if traffic was flowing, even if the light was green. Like a bee drawn to honey, Bugs would slow to a crawl and somehow engineer himself into a red light. If there were eight signals along the journey, Bugs would routinely, as a matter of course, catch all eight red lights. Cars around him would panic discovering who their neighbour was, knowing fully well that they'd be the victim of red signal after red signal simply by virtue of their chance association with Bugs and Pratibha.

Apart from theatre, Karl and Kunal were soon introduced to an art that they were both soon to excel at, an art for which their passion and commitment could hardly be questioned. The art of drinking.

It all happened the weekend before opening night. After a successful technical rehearsal, Pearl organized an impromptu party at her place. The night kicked off with a spectacular round of awards, which included awards for:

(a) The most inattentive actor—Karl
(b) The most argumentative actor—Bugs
(c) The actor who coughed through other actors' lines—Kunal
(d) The punctuality award to the actor who came on time twice in 40 rehearsals—Baba

The awards varied from a used tissue to half a blueberry muffin. This set the tone for the evening. It was then that Karl and Kunal stumbled upon what would become one of the greatest influences of their life so far—Jell-o shots. The Jell-o shot was invented by the German genius Lionel Hartinger who while trying to invent a washing machine using two dinner plates and no soap, and increasingly became so frustrated that he turned to mixing drinks in a big way.

Hartinger decided to forego the golden rule of mixing alcohol, that is you never mix your green alcohol with your blue. Soon, one thing led to another, after all nothing can be more dangerous than a lonely super-genius inventor who is completely plastered, and to feed his hunger, he combined a complex carbohydrate, jelly, with a simple carbohydrate, his neighbours' vodka. The result was the Jell-o shot, fourth in the list of the twentieth century's top inventions, just below the computer, the automobile, and the TV remote, and just above scabies and dengue fever.

Today, the Jell-o shot is used for a very virtuous purpose—to get unseasoned female drinkers drunk fast, so that they may be taken advantage of. Two Jell-o shots are normally enough to make a girl feel that any boy's a young Marlon Brando. By contrast, four Jell-os will make the boy feel like he's the old Marlon Brando, and should never be administered.

On their virgin Jell-o night, Kunal had six recorded Jell-o shots and seven unrecorded. Karl topped this number by two. The result? By the end of the night, Karl was in just his underwear, asking a potted plant to go for a drive with him. Kunal was almost unconscious, insisting he wasn't really a potted plant. Until then, the boys had drunk alcohol occasionally, but this was the first time that they had actually drunk the entire Indian Ocean. It was not to be the last time either.

The feeling you get on the opening night of a new play cannot be easily explained to males. It is like the feeling a pregnant woman gets when her water breaks. The difference is that, generally, after her water breaks she delivers the baby and the worst is behind her. Here, from the time you wake up that morning till the show actually gets under way, you remain in an agitated, exaggeratedly pained state. At the end of the show, of course, it's normally the audience who find themselves in that state, and therein lies the beauty of theatre.

For Karl, the morning was no different. He couldn't understand why he had this electric current coursing through his body. Alarmed, he called out to Kunal, and Kunal who generally needed five cups of coffee just to stand up was in an even more agitated state. He hadn't slept at all that night, and was sweating from every conceivable orifice, but at different speeds.

The best thing to do was to head to the theatre. Things got off to a good start. A quick rehearsal, sound checks, and then lunch. The sound check as mentioned before is unique to urban India. Generally, a non-English-speaking assistant to the director of sound (in this case, Pia) tests the microphone. This he does (and this is copied by every sound guy all over India without a single change) by saying the magic words, 'Mic check,' followed by, '1, 2.' The more experienced ones take this routine a little further, 'Mic check, 1, 2, 3...' Repeat, 'Mic check, 1, 2, 3...' And finally, 'Check, check, che...ck.' The last couple of times, the word is delivered as if it is in French—in a soothing, soft lilt. 'Che...ck, che...ck.' Why this is so, no one can tell, but the whole process is reproduced, without exception, across the country.

Lunch options were quite varied. You had the chicken roll, the mince roll, or the veg roll. In all three preparations, the main artiste was the mayonnaise and the chicken, mince, and veggies had a brief cameo.

As the seven o'clock bell rang, the performers gathered in a dressing room for a quick motivational speech from Pearl, which ended with her customary, 'Don't behave like complete idiots' refrain, and then a quick prayer. After this, the huddle was formed. Well before cricket and rugby teams practised the huddle, it existed in Mumbai's theatre circuit. In this version, all performers grab one another's shoulders, and standing in a semicircle, bang their feet and shout gibberish, 'Otagootaootaboota yehyehyoooo...!' Mind you, they had some highly educated people in their troupe, two MBAs, one LLB, one PhD student, and a computer engineer. However, all thought it prudent to cry out, 'Oootagootaootaboota yehyehyoooo.' It always caused an explosion of energy, and soon the troupe was pumped up, perhaps more than may have been necessary for a musical about the life of Jesus Christ.

The play began with Karl entering from the audience in a brown toga, carrying a bowl of holy water (or as he liked to stress, water from the men's changing room), singing the opening song. This was a solo performance and the song was remarkable in that it had only one line, just the single lyric, 'Prepare ye the way of the Lord, prepare ye the way of the Lord, prepare ye the way of the Lord, prepare ye the way of the Lord'...you get the drift. On opening night, as Karl walked through the audience, he quickly realized that the majority of the audience didn't actually want to be baptized. In fact, the majority of the audience didn't seem to want any exposure to water. Karl quickly made a mental note not to sprinkle water from the second show onwards. Okay, maybe just on the cheaper seats. As he reached the front of the audience, Karl now almost in a trance, didn't see a leg extended into the aisle and tripped and fell. The water splashed on to Mr and Mrs Chaudhury, the invited VIP guests, as they had sponsored the clothes. Ironically, the Chaudhurys, dressed in all their finery but now doused in holy water, were rushed backstage where they were given a wide range of dry clothes to choose from—a red toga, a blue toga, a green toga, a brown toga, and a toga of suspect colour. Once again, the irony of swapping a fancy suit for a green toga was not lost on anyone backstage, as the Chaudhurys themselves had stitched the togas in the first place.

Of course, the audience thought it was part of the act and applauded the Chaudhurys. Buoyed by their reaction, Karl continued with his one-line song and finally walked on to the stage where, in a riot of colours, all the performers joined him for the last verse of the song, which went exactly like the rest of the song, 'Prepare ye the way of the Lord, prepare ye the way of the Lord, prepare ye the way of the Lord, prepare ye the way of the Lord.' The show went off well. Kunal's crippled dancing was one of the highlights, but keep in mind that the audience was filled with invitees, friends and family, and people who had worked on the show.

There was a momentary crisis when Bugs entered as Jesus. Immediately, whispers and catcalls could be heard: 'Oh my God! He's too fat to be Jesus,' 'That can't be Jesus,' 'Jesus! That isn't Jesus,' 'Jesus Christ,' or the one that stayed with Karl forever, 'In Jesus' time, no one was that fat.' This was one of the main reasons the play didn't have a long run. Karl learnt quickly that in India there are some things you don't tinker with and Jesus is one of them.

Karl and Kunal were also exposed to an audience for the first time. Two things a Mumbai audience does, that are a real challenge for actors to handle, are 'the cough' and 'the shift'. The 'cough' is never performed by anyone who genuinely has a cough. It is started by an alpha cougher, who gives it an honest go and then immediately clears his throat, holding his notes with the precision of a Carnatic vocalist. The clearing of the throat, rather than the cough itself, is the loudest sound. Now a peculiar phenomenon occurs. Suddenly, the alpha cougher is followed by other coughers, some single, some in unison. The technique remains the same—a cough followed by a clearing of the throat. During the opening night, Karl and Kunal witnessed this cough wave first-hand. The song on stage was drowned out completely, and the non-coughing members of the audience were mesmerized by the coughers, each of whom did an excellent job.

The other thing the boys noticed was the shifting. This was done mainly by the male members of the audience (if you'll excuse the pun) who seemed to have a hands-on approach to their groins. They repeatedly touched that area of the body and did a little gardening. This was also known by its Russian name, 'perestroika', which means 'restructuring'. The reasons for this behaviour cannot be confirmed. Some seem to do it because they just want to check whether everything is still there. Some do it because everyone else is doing it. Some do it because they want a full-bodied experience in the theatre. And why should the experience in the theatre be confined only to the region of the neck upwards? The boys also noticed that during the shifting procedure, men never, repeat, never used both hands. One hand alone would do all the running up and down, the other would never get started. It was like two political parties, one running the country from day to day, while the other sat in opposition, never bothering to help out.

At the end of the show, it was all worth it. Karl instantly understood what was meant by the thrill of the theatre, why professionals took time off to pursue an art form that offered no money and almost no visibility, why a group of diverse people would go that extra yard to perform a play. The answer most definitely was free drinks. Free drinks and really oily kebabs. The opening night was celebrated with the biggest drinking binge of Karl's life. Till today, he can't recall a thing about that night, and thankfully he was asleep at six o'clock in the morning when his father woke him up. Their conversation went something like this:

Jehaan: Son, did you have a nice opening night?

Karl: Yeah.

Jehaan: Then why are you sleeping on an Ambassador?

Karl was found asleep on top of an Ambassador car by his father, while the latter was walking the dog. He intuitively knew then that he really should go and watch his son's play.

College was also the time for experimenting with clothes. St Xavier's had long been declared both by the UNESCO and the UN as the centre or bastion of fashion in India. Kunal and Karl spent the first few weeks staring with wonder. There were men wearing berets who, they found out later, weren't actually watchmen at all. Then there was a group of supremely vain and materialistic women who wore very little material whatsoever. But Karl and Kunal were intrinsically drawn to another powerful force—shorts. Shorts were soon to become the single biggest influence in their lives. Both in college and at rehearsals, they saw people in shorts. The shorts came in three sizes: (a) the really short shorts or wrist bands, (b) the medium shorts, and (c) the long shorts that stopped short two inches from the ankles. The third they rejected as a pair of shorts with a complex, a complex of wanting to be a pair of trousers.

Kunal continued experimenting with his shorts, which ultimately looked like a ribbon around a penguin. Karl went for the medium-sized shorts that had the added advantage of many pockets. Years of unemployment had taught Karl a valuable lesson. One of the biggest problems encountered in a social situation other than oily hair and body odour was what to do with one's hands. The right-sized pockets immediately came to the rescue. Karl also hit on another device he was to use to his advantage socially—he found that in any lonely, awkward public situation, he could easily spend twelve minutes effortlessly pretending to search for something in all six pockets. This helped kill time and gave him a less awkward presence at bus stops and railway stations, for one. He tried teaching Kunal this ruse, but Kunal's hands were too ungainly. He made a complete mess of the pocket presentation and often came out looking like a man putting on a big act. The two boys learnt another very important lesson here—that Karl was more comfortable and convincing at being genuine with insincere actions. Kunal on the other hand wasn't.

They got a nod of approval when Pearl vouched for their dress sense one day with, 'Okay you two imbeciles. I guarantee you, in those shorts, no girl will ever want to be seen out with you twice.'

College and theatre rolled on. One day, while trying to bend his fingernail backward without using any other finger for support, Karl felt something fall on his head. It turned out to be Pearl's hand, which kept slapping the back of his head repeatedly, and not very gently either. She was trying to introduce him to Mumbai theatre's grand impresario, Hosi Vasunia. Hosi was a large, loud, and forthright man with utterly deadpan delivery and the occasional temper. Hosi said, 'I'm told you like to speak a mile a minute. Well, there's a guy who's started a radio channel who you may want to meet.'

Karl entered through a large door, which led to a room that was, quite astonishingly, smaller than the door. In it sat a pleasant-looking gentleman who said in a voice smaller than the room, 'I'll take your voice test. Just pretend you're a guitar or a drum roll.' He then proceeded to make the most infantile of noises. First he presented some chang, chang, chang, ting aling, ting aling guitar sounds, then proceeded to his version of the piano, which was based loosely on a mouse's death throes after being run over by a car. The car itself was emulated by his flute solo. The drums sounded like a man spending far too much time in the toilet, and when he threatened to become a human violin, Karl thought it prudent to butt in and remind him that it was Karl himself who needed to give the audition.

Depressed that he wasn't able to present his pièce de résistance, the harmonica minuet, the gentleman glumly pressed a few buttons in a detached manner, and then in a barely audible monotone, tinged with resentment and latent ferocity, he said, 'Okay, it's recording.' Karl, as was his wont, gave his voice free rein for what he thought was three and a half hours but was told later was actually nine minutes, fifteen seconds.

When Karl finished, he looked up at the engineer who by then looked extremely forlorn. 'Bas, that's enough,' he said. 'We only need 30 seconds of voice.' Karl didn't care. His mind was occupied by far more sophisticated thoughts like when it might be a good time to organize the next piss-up or how delectable Pia's curves were. So when Hosi enquired about the audition, he made the universal sign of failure—a forefinger forming a cutting action on the throat followed by two fingers squeezing the nose, a wrist slapping each opposite shoulder, and three hippy-hippy shakes.

Hosi said, 'Wrong answer, my friend. You've been selected as a disc jockey for Radio Star. But there's some good news and some bad news. The good news is that your pay packet will be 3,000 rupees a month (that is equivalent to approximately 10,000 rupees, or two hamburgers today); the bad news is you've got the 6 am slot four times a week.'

Karl felt a curious sense of ambivalence. Still, 3,000 rupees was a lot of money for a teenager. But what the hell? How in the world did he survive that audition? I mean, had they lost the tape? It was only later, much later, that he was told he got selected because of a very simple principle—no other person had shown up. As the one-legged dancer Shin Van put it, 'The best way to win a race is to be the only runner.'

Due to the five o'clock wake-up call, Karl discovered one of God's angels without whom most of society would be unable to function. Coffee. Karl realized that to go against one's better instinct and report for work on time, modern man needed a stimulant. Since most companies did not permit drugs or alcohol on their premises before 6 pm, coffee would have to do.

The radio shows went live at 6 am, a time which generally ensured a listenership of three, sometimes two if Karl's dad fell back asleep. The location was the AIR Studios (no one has ever really found out what AIR stands for; it probably means 'All Inside Retired') at Churchgate.

The AIR Studios operated on three simple maxims:
(1) The studio may or may not be open at 6 am
(2) Which means the studio would, more likely, be open at 7 am
(3) Just to be on the safe side, don't show up at the studio before 8:30 am

The studio was owned by the Government of India. Only they had the key. However, no one in India knew who the Government of India was. Most Indians hadn't ever heard of them. Furthermore, they didn't seem to have an address or phone number where they could be reminded to bring the key to the studio on time.

Very often, this meant that Karl would find himself

waiting outside the studio, while his live show was supposed to be on air. Hence, most of his shows, instead of beginning with the traditional greeting, 'Good Morning Mumbai,' would begin with: 'Sorry, but the Government of India couldn't be located…' This unusual salutation caught on, and soon became a preferred mode of greeting among many of Mumbai's citizens.

Karl had two shows—one was a dial-in phone show and the other was an interview/request show with a celebrity. The latter soon became an interview/request show with the cousin of the celebrity, and later the neighbour of the celebrity's cousin, as they ran out of genuine celebrities willing to appear on the show by week four. This was because of two reasons—no one thought radio was a serious enough medium, unless of course you were a cricket score, which most celebrities were not. Second, no real celebrity woke up before 12:45 in the afternoon, which meant she'd only be able to do the live 6 am show at roughly 3 pm. This was late even by AIR's generous standards.

On the dial-in show, Karl would get all sorts of questions. The most common ones were, 'My dog has too many fleas, what should I do?', 'My girlfriend's name is Purvi, but she doesn't know who I am, what should I do?', 'I'm in love with a girl who lives in New Delhi who I've never met and is probably 73 years old. What should I do?', or the perennial, 'In the song "Alice", can you please, please tell me who the fuck is Alice?'

Karl's only thought through all these routine requests was that when he became Station Manager someday, he'd definitely relax the drinking policy.

The first celebrity he met was Gary Lawyer. Gary had the best singing voice in India, and probably the tightest pair of jeans. His twin passions were music and bikes. His favourite quote was from the great French freedom writer Jean-Jacques Rousseau (pet name, Monty), who famously said in 1786 that he'd much rather spend time on a motorbike than on a woman.

Now Gary turned out to be very friendly. Like most great musicians, he ended all his sentences with three shakes of his head. This could go up to four if he was getting a trifle animated. He also ran his fingers through the back of his hair in what was subtly an all-out effort to get the locks to grow longer. All these eccentricities disappeared when he sang. No one could deny that he was a brilliant singer. Karl took an instant liking to Gary and, as a mark of respect, and as a tribute to Gary Lawyer, Karl started wearing shirts that were one size too tight for him. Gary couldn't have asked for more from his new disciple. His forays into radio and theatre improved Karl's profile—as Snow White famously told one of her seven dwarfs, 'A little celebrity goes a long way in a big college.'

chapter 5

It was in Russian class that Karl came across someone who he initially thought was a Polish car salesman, Stanislavski. This error was later rectified and Stanislavski, though dead for a hundred years, regained his original status as the father of the method school of acting. This is not to be confused with the Methodist school, which is also about acting but is helped along by dollops of religion and is far more popular.

Fascinated by all the talk of sense memories, impulse acting, being in the moment, and pictures of large-chested Russian actresses from earlier centuries, Karl and Kunal researched and studied all they could about 'the method'. They did this by having a conversation with the Russian teacher.

Karl and Kunal: Where does one study the method?

Russian teacher: In an acting studio.

Karl and Kunal: Where can one find an acting studio?

Russian teacher: Go straight, then turn left from Canada to a place near 14th and Lexington in New York.

Karl and Kunal: What's the place called?

Russian teacher: The Lee Strasburg Acting Studio.

The boys decided that the moment they graduated

from college, they would go to the Lee Strasburg Studio to improve their craft. Of course, passing from the arts stream in college was a ridiculous affair. You could not fail even if you tried. There was no recorded failure by anyone who actually sat for an exam. The only way you'd fail would be by not turning up.

By now, Karl and Kunal had had their fair share of Pias and Tanyas, Amritas and Shaheens. They were thirsty, thirsty for new knowledge, thirsty for the American 'school' of acting, but thirstiest for American girls.

From childhood, Indian boys develop a rather fixed idea about American girls. This largely consists of three or four irrefutable points: (a) American girls are nymphomaniacs, (b) the moment you land in America they jump on you and molest you, (c) the molestation goes on for months, and (d) the molesting normally occurs in crowded places like main streets, where if you dare complain to anyone, you are molested by that person as well.

Lee Strasburg offered two courses: one was a fourteen-week course, the other a nine-month one. Karl and Kunal decided to opt for the fourteen-week one. It was cheaper. Maria set them up with an ex-advertising colleague friend of theirs, Anilbhai. Thus the stay would be free. Indeed, there is no other place like a fellow Indian's, particularly when the lodgings offered are free. This is why even head honchos of big companies like the Tatas and Birlas are known to stay with friends and family when abroad.

Karl and Kunal hadn't been as far as Andheri, let alone America, but first there were some loose ends to be tied up. Karl said his goodbyes to Pia, although

100

the relationship had declined, and he promised to be good. Pia in turn warned him to watch out for the notorious American girls. 'The moment you arrive in America, they will molest you. They are sex-crazy maniacs. They will molest you for months, and if you can't handle it and dare to complain to anybody…' By now Karl wasn't listening; he was already in Brooklyn's Brighton Beach, New York, with 57 American beauties in various stages of undress, fulfilling his every need and then some.

The two friends set out for New York on a British Airways plane on a warm September night. Never really having travelled by air before, they were unprepared for much of what they encountered on the flight. The first thing they heard was a gaggle of geese cackling at the top of their voices. A second glance revealed that it was a Gujarati family of seventeen, en route New Jersey via New York. Although they sat beside one another, they all spoke as if they were on stage, projecting their voices to the balcony. It was as fine a piece of theatre as one could have seen. It was evident from their conversation that they didn't trust American food and had brought their own dhoklas and theplas with plenty of pickles. The food was then distributed in what can only be described as a rugby scrummage. Hands and legs went flying in different directions as food was arranged and rearranged, then passed to one another. Right in the middle of this feeding frenzy, right in the epicentre of the ravenous pack, sat our two terrified friends. They would have to endure this for 22 hours.

As far as Kunal could see, there were no sex-crazy

American women on the plane. In fact, the only person with blonde hair turned out to be a male Indian music student off to Berkeley. Apparently he had coloured his hair in an effort to fit in. Which is roughly the same as wearing your hair in the Rastafarian style when you're off to meet the Dalai Lama.

The Gujarati onslaught continued. Airline help was summoned in true Indian style, with the two-finger snap, or with 'Tch'—the Indian equivalent of 'Will you attend to me?' While Westerners on flights tend to waste their breath on 'Excuse me please, sorry to bother you', Indians settle for a simple 'Eh', snap, 'Tch', or 'A'.

Karl was confounded by the amenities of the economy class. Today it's an open secret that economy class seats were designed to fit seven-year-olds. For a first-time flyer, these obvious facts were not quite so obvious. In their row of four seats chained together, Kunal occupied the end seat, a rather malnourished gentleman the other extreme seat, and bang in the middle was Karl and the malnourished man's missus, certainly the largest living creature Karl had ever seen. Suddenly it became patently obvious why the malnourished man was quite so malnourished; someone was clearly eating a little extra. Karl had always thought of Indian women as the most beautiful in the world; but when an Indian woman gets fat, the country doesn't seem quite large enough. She went by the unassuming name of Janaki, and Karl thought to himself that perhaps only a career in wrestling might suit her. Soon, Janaki took their relationship to the next level. Unknown to the airline, Janaki had brought two guests along with her—her hips. She deposited one on her fragile husband's lap, who emitted a groan of fear mixed with a token disapproval. The second, and Karl would swear the larger one, she pushed into the safe confines of Karl's lap.

This was done deftly, in one sweeping motion, as the hip came alive with a mind of its own, in a bundle of flowing protoplasm, pushed Karl's hand disdainfully off the seat's armrest and landed with one fell swoop on his lap. Kunal couldn't quite tell which was quivering more, the personified protoplasm or Karl. Worse was to follow. Forms had to be filled on board. These forms were in English and neither Janaki nor her hips spoke English. Well, that's not strictly true. Janaki's knowledge of the English language was contained in her controlled but flexible use of the word 'vegetarian'. For instance, when asked by a crew member if she was Indian, she answered, 'Vegetarian.' When asked her destination, she replied, 'Vegetarian.' When asked her sleeping husband's name, once again the reply was an assured, confident, 'Vegetarian.'

So when the white forms appeared, she looked at Karl, handed her form to him like a child who has just completed her exam paper and said 'Vegetarian.' To get her off his back, or more appropriately to get her hip off his lap, Karl decided to fill in her form for her. After hours spent negotiating for her passport and visa (how do these guys get their visas so easily?), he could tell she was pleased with the result, although it was hard to gauge from her reaction, which was the expected, 'Vegetarian.'

Predictably enough, when the meal tray came, she cried 'Vegetarian, vegetarian, vegetarian!' until she went hoarse. Obviously, someone had warned her about the food. Strangely, no one from the Gujarati group offered her any of their choice snacks. Karl couldn't help feeling it had something to do with the fact that she could eat all they had in one go, if she chose.

JFK airport astounded the boys. Having been exposed only to Sahar airport, and one corner of Frankfurt airport, JFK came as a complete shock.

Karl: You'd expect an airport with just three letters in its name to be a little smaller.

Kunal: Okay, by my watch, we've been in America for seven minutes now, so where are the women?

It was true; seven minutes had passed and they were frozen. Fairly close by, they could see Janaki arguing with a staff member who was trying to help her with a connecting flight, but there seemed to be no middle point between Chicago and Vegetarian. The futile argument continued. Karl and Kunal were awestruck by the mass of people, signs, machinery, and the sheer size of the airport.

At the immigration counter, a brusque African American woman of ample proportions barked, 'Erich from?'

Karl replied, 'No, Karl Marshall.'

This produced an even more curt tone, 'Erich human?'

'Er…no, my name is Karl…'

She snapped at him furiously: 'ERICH FROM!' This time, it wasn't even a question.

Karl tried to speak, but his voice and courage both failed him. He tried to whisper the magic word, 'Vegetarian', but to no avail.

104

Meanwhile, the woman's head was snapping back and forth like a giant toy. 'ERICH FROM? ERICH FROM?'

A voice from the darkness advised Karl, 'She wants to know where you are from, show her your passport.'

Kunal tried to pacify Karl by saying Janaki was probably next in the queue.

Karl and Kunal may as well have been on another planet. Coming from Mumbai where everybody stared at you, they suddenly found themselves in a huge space where people, many of them over seven feet tall, flew about doing their own thing at ninety miles per hour and speaking in strange accents with harsh tones. The boys were so intimidated that they almost held hands. And where were the women? Where were the sex maniacs they had been promised? The only woman they had interacted with so far had ben the rude one at immigration and, well, Janaki, who from a respectable distance could only loosely, very loosely, be termed female.

The boys followed Maria's instructions to the letter. On reaching the house where Anilbhai lived, they were to take a key from the doorman after showing him their passports. However, the burly West Indian doorman who went by the name 'Sugar' waved away the documents and gave them the key directly.

Kunal: What a city, Karl; either there's too much checking or no checking at all.

Anilbhai lived on the third floor of a pokey sort of building. He was at work when the boys entered their new home. They were greeted by two rooms, each the size of an earbud box. One of the rooms had an open bed. When the boys woke up, Anilbhai was standing before them. He had the smallest face and feet the boys had ever seen, and looked like a jackfruit with legs attached. Like the Sphinx, Anilbhai was both old and had never really smiled. 'You are in my room, go there,' he offered by way of greeting, slamming the door in their embarrassed faces. Karl and Kunal's only thought was, 'Let's go home, even the Indians are monsters here.'

Anilbhai was a strange kettle of fish. First, what kind of person has only one name? Very few can pull it off. God definitely, Elvis maybe, Vyjayantimala sure, but Anilbhai? He looked and sounded like unfinished business. And as the boys found out after Karl asked Anilbhai if he'd like some ketchup, and Kunal said there was a telephone call for him, he was one of those people who communicated in the old-fashioned way—using grunts, growls, and all sorts of other inarticulate guttural sounds.

Anilbhai never asked about Karl's parents. He never asked what the boys were doing in America. He never asked anything. Maybe he did, but his language of grunts and growls was difficult to comprehend. The two boys didn't like the vibes in the house. Things took a turn for the worse when Anilbhai brought his girlfriend over for the weekend. Susan was 40 something, modelled genetically after a stick, and was always difficult to understand as she swallowed the end of her sentences, so you'd have to try and decipher what she was saying from the first half. Conversations between the two were a sheer delight to witness, and the boys listened awestruck.

Susan: What should we do tonight…[inaudible murmur]
Anilbhai: (Grunt)
Susan: But that may finish off…[inaudible murmur]
Anilbhai: (Growl)
Susan: Let's ask the boys. Boys….[inaudible question]
Anilbhai: (Growl)

Karl and Kunal froze at the possible implications of the request, for there was clearly a request here. But they were certain that no one in the wide world could decipher what exactly was being asked for. They needed to quit this forum of progressive communication, and fast.

Soon, the boys began their course. Somewhere on 14th Street and Something stood the Lee Strasburg Studio. As the boys entered, they were conscious that they were following in the footsteps of all-time greats like Marlon Brando, Sydney Poitier, and Paul Newman. However, as everyone spoke Spanish and was clearly from Cuba, they realized they must have accidentally stumbled upon the Cuban Embassy, which was also known for its high acting standards in those days. The matter was soon cleared up. They were in fact at the Lee Strasburg Acting Studio, and only the front desk functioned occasionally as the Cuban Embassy. After the traditional welcome, handshakes, and pictures, the boys were given their schedule for the next fourteen weeks.

Kunal drank in the number of pretty women passing by, and noted sadly how none made a beeline for either of them. People often ask what makes America great. What distinguishes America from India? Now there are a number of answers to this, such as (a) India has more cows, cows in India have more rights, and (b) America has less cows, cows here have fewer rights. This is primarily because Americans eat cows, thereby swallowing their rights. There are other more subtle differences, e.g. Americans can eat while standing, and Indians can spell words like 'colour' and 'flavour' correctly. In America, Mississippi is a river, in India she's a married Sindhi lady. Americans love coming to India, Indians love not returning from America. Americans invented computers, Indians evolved into computers. The list goes on and on. Yet, if there is just one primary difference that we're looking for, it is this: in the American education system, you get to choose, mix, and match your classes according to your convenience. This is the principal reason why America's progress has recently been thwarted, and here I quote the Dean of Belmont Abbey College, North Carolina: 'Us damn Americans take too Godawful long to finish our classes.'

The two boys were stunned at their good fortune. They used McEwen's Formula to choose their classes— 'No class before breakfast and none after lunch.' This creates a window of just 10 am to 1 pm—simply put, a three-hour day. McEwen, by the way, is 63 years old today, and is yet to complete his primary education.

The boys at the acting studios often covered for one another by opting for the same classes. The only dispute was over the tai chi and yoga classes. Both these involved assuming postures that you could never display publicly. Also, the boys could never quite decide which of the two involved less work. The matter was put to rest by attending both classes, and yoga won hands and feet down. It was observed that yoga allowed for a lot of time on one's back. Tai chi not only kept you on your feet but occasionally insisted that you use just one of them.

The first class they went to was an acting class taught by a gentleman called Warwick Castle, and indeed there is a famous castle at Warwick. Warwick could easily have been mistaken for an owl in his younger days; he was all eyes. The super-large eyes dominated his face and ensured that his other features went unnoticed. Castle paired off the class. Kunal was paired with an Israeli girl called Eliza, and Karl with a Mexican boy called Jorge. The pairs were all given written scenes to act out. Kunal, like most Indian males tend to do, fell in love with Eliza immediately, as she was the first 'foreign female' he had seriously interacted with. It helped that theirs was a love scene from the Dennis McIntyre play *Modigliani*. Karl, however, had a distinct disadvantage. It wasn't that the piece was an extract from the screenplay of *Rocky 1*. It was, in fact, that his co-actor didn't speak a word of English. Finally, Jorge had to wing it. While Karl read out Rocky's lines correctly, Jorge who was playing Rocky's coach made do with just one-word replies, 'Rocky', 'Er...Rocky', 'Er...Rocky', 'Er...Rocky'.

Castle's class was relaxed and friendly. Students ate and drank throughout. Some came late, a couple left early. A beautiful Swedish girl had her feet on the desk. Karl couldn't believe it. Why the hell didn't he go to a school like this back home? And to top it all, instead of algebra, you had to learn *Rocky*!

Next up was the world of sense memory. Sense

memory was the most important part of the method. Let's do a comparison with the human body. If the human body was the method then sense memory was the eyes, nose, ears, tongue, one lung, the odd kidney, two patellas, a femur, and probably a large chunk of the heart. Here, you were encouraged to play out your impulses. Then you combined your bleeding impulses, which the sense memory recalled, such as impulses you felt when remembering an old lover's perfume or your grandfather's bad breath, whichever was stronger. There was nothing wrong with the thinking, it was the process that was the problem. The sense memory class was held in the largest hall, and the teacher was a rather beautiful lady called Jenny. Kunal, who in his imagination, already mated with eight foreign students in the school, immediately wanted to marry her, and promptly beget four children, no less.

For the first few minutes, all the actors were encouraged to shout, scream, and jump up and down; in other words, to behave exactly as if they were in Parliament. All the nervous energy could be eliminated through such activity, and only after its elimination could a person truly relax and attend to his art form. It was while doing this that Karl, who was swinging his arms like King Louie from the *Jungle Book*, came into contact with a Norwegian boy called Joachim. And by contact I mean his swinging hand slapped Joachim's face. This resulted in an absolute breakdown of the peace process between Norway and India. Soon, the two were wrestling on the floor in a scene Kunal later thought was highly reminiscent of *Kramer vs Kramer*. Jennifer sent both boys out to cool down.

Karl couldn't believe it. No punishment, no reprimand, just five minutes to 'cool off' and they were back in class. The American way of doing things was just great! Better still, having cooled down, Joachim was quick to apologize and the two became good friends, which was most useful because having a Scandinavian friend meant that he would eventually lead one to the best thing about Scandinavia—its women.

At the end of day one Karl, Kunal, and Joachim had lunch together at a nearby diner. They were joined by Joachim's fellow Norwegian, the absolutely stunning Elka. By now, Kunal was in much the same state as an adolescent dog who would mount just about anything—a lamp, a table leg, a pillar, a bedpost. One look at Elka was almost enough for him to wet himself. But it was Karl who moved quickly, like a falcon pouncing on a rabbit.

While extending his arm to shake Elka's hand, Karl spilled some coffee on her white shirt. In less than a second, sixteen pairs of eager male hands appeared with napkins, volunteering to wipe off the coffee. Elka lazily asked Karl to do the honours. Karl decided that the action must be executed slowly, so that he could savour the moment.

Elka, Kunal, Joachim, and Karl soon became good friends. Sparks began to fly between Elka and Karl, and even more sparks flew between Kunal and every passing female of any age, shape, or colour. Karl realized that the classes were going to be great fun, and everything would be just fine, but for that damn man with the single name—Anilbhai.

Strasburg had a bulletin board on which ads could

be placed for rooms to rent, appliances, clothes, and the like. The Anilbhai problem was solved when they met a Greek–Australian boy called Yaani. Yaani advertised for three roommates to split a studio apartment on 6th Broadway, but it was what he put in brackets that won Karl and Kunal over and identified Yaani as the perfect roommate for them. Beside the address of the studio apartment, in large brackets were the words, 'Right Next to the Porno Sector'. 'An actor after my heart,' sighed Karl.

Within a few hours, four boys from overseas were sharing an apartment in Manhattan—Yaani, Karl, Kunal, and an investment banker called Aadith. When Karl and Kunal went to Anilbhai to convey the good news, his response was predictable—a growl followed by an almost inaudible, 'Hurry up.'

The new apartment was right next to the Aues Dueux Treaux restaurant, which the boys later discovered was either the name of the richest man in France or the numbers '1, 2, 3' in French. Living together was a whole new experience—it is an unstated fact that when unsupervised young males share an apartment, both their emotions and their hygiene are severely challenged.

The apartment itself was an apartment only in name. It consisted of two small adjacent rooms, with about three square feet set aside for the kitchen, and a single, tiny bathroom. This meant it was either you and the oven or you and the fridge in there at one time. It could never be you, the oven, and the fridge.

Yaani and Aadith shared one room, which had a 600-year-old bed that had last been dusted by

Christopher Columbus himself in 1493. Karl and Kunal found two aerobic mats in the other room; this ensured that they never actually slept on the ground but in fact were almost a half inch above the floor. The combined rent for the apartment was $600 a month, effectively $150 per head. But not even $15,000 would have been penalty enough for the bathroom experience. The boys adjusted to a spirit of healthy competition every morning. Everyone wanted the first use of the wicket. Invariably, Aadith's alarm would go off first.

Aadith was an unkempt, burly Tam Bram boy from Chennai, with the straightest hair possible. This was partly due to the fact that he applied 33 litres of oil to his scalp every single night. Aadith's other striking feature was that he was part grizzly bear, and hair grew from every part of him. Karl remembered being horrified at seeing clumps of hair on Aadith's forehead and knuckles, and also the undersides of his arms where human beings don't generally experience much hair growth. Only primates, the praying mantis, and a few females of the species grow hair in those places. Since Aadith wasn't a primate or a female, the general consensus was that he was a rather fat specimen of a praying mantis.

Aadith was always up before 6 am, and would rush to the bathroom and begin the massacre. As he had to reach Goldman Sachs by 7 am, he would turn into a veritable whirlwind in the toilet. The shave, the shower, the deposit, and what hardly passed for oral hygiene had to be finished in thirteen minutes. The result was clumps of hair on the floor, on the pot seat, on the wall, in the shower, on the door handle and, worst of all, in the washbasin, where they formed an effective anti-drainage system.

The next batsman in was Karl who did his best to repair the damage, but toilet paper can only do so much. The only way to deal with the situation was to get out as soon as possible. Next in was Yaani whose sanguine approach to life allowed him to place his eleven assorted hair products neatly in the inferno that was their toilet. Unaffected by all evidence of Aadith and Karl's innings, he added to the damage with blithe unconcern. Invariably, Kunal was the last man in. To be the last one to use the toilet is to draw the short end of the stick. To him went the honour of drinking in the sights, sounds, smells, and residues of his three companions. Sometimes, Kunal could actually be heard sobbing inside. After all, growing up in Mumbai, he had never really had to share a toilet and had never been subject to this relentless assault on the senses.

The other problem area for the boys was food. Between the four of them, they could cook very little, effectively disproving the 'too many cooks' myth. None of them could actually make broth. So they simply brought street food home. It was in this apartment that Karl and Kunal witnessed several modern-day miracles that reaffirmed their belief in God and all things supernatural.

The first and the most serious was when Karl fell asleep with an unfinished, open bag of crisps by his side, yet amazingly, eight hours later, the crisps were still as edible and as fresh. Such a thing would have been unthinkable in India. Then there was the matter of drinking water. On one particular day, the boys ran out of drinking water. Yaani quietly turned on a tap in the kitchen (used by former tenants to wash their dishes) and lapped the water directly from the tap. Imagine drinking tap water in India, imagine drinking any water in India that has not been boiled three times, and then filtered four times, and finally purified five times. Unthinkable. For days, they monitored Yaani's health for any signs of impending death, such as acne or diarrhoea, but nothing happened. Buoyed by this miracle, Karl and Kunal started drinking water from all the taps in the apartment. They also started taking photographic evidence of the miracle to display back in Mumbai. Till today, both are very proud of pictures showing them consuming water from a tap in the toilet. Proof of the unconquerable, intrepid spirit of the Indian traveller who fought stout-heartedly against all the evils of a New York apartment and lived to tell the tale.

They were soon to find New York had much more to offer than just drinking water—guns, traffic cops, and supermarkets were all to play a part.

The relaxed atmosphere in the acting studio meant Karl and Kunal started treating the whole New York experience as a holiday. They found the city streets invigorating and exciting and occasionally very long. One evening, while returning late from the acting studio, they passed a house that had someone who looked like Elton John in a white suit sprawled outside it. They crawled closer, only to discover that what they thought was the 'Crocodile Rock' singer was actually a big white mattress. On even closer inspection of Elton, they realized the red embroidery they had spied from afar was a series of really large bloodstains. The two boys looked at each other, since there was no one else around. Karl gingerly turned the mattress over with his feet. Elton's back didn't have any stains on it and was a pristine white, which is how both boys would have liked to remember him. Sleeping on half-inch thick aerobic mats hurt both the ego and the body. Elton John was the ticket to a better nocturnal life. They quietly folded the large mattress into an accordion and marched with it towards the nearest tube station. The bloodstained torso of Elton John was thus hidden from the eye. Only in New York can two Indian boys carry a large bloodstained mattress on the subway and not get so much as a second glance from a stranger.

Back at the apartment, Yaani's scientific mind suggested: 'Instead of trying to take the bloodstains off Elton, just turn it over so that they're hidden by the floor.' And so it came to pass that on their remaining nights in New York City, Karl and Kunal slept with Elton John.

Crossing Washington Square Park one evening, an extremely large African American man stopped them. Always the sensible one, Karl made sure Kunal was between him and the large man in case things took a turn for the worse. 'You guys wanna buy a piece?' Somehow, this was more an order than a question. Under his jacket, he quickly showed them four or five different kinds of handguns. As their blood froze, Kunal recalled some sage advice offered to him in

Mumbai, 'Always try to agree with a street tough.' Trying not to disappoint the gruff giant, Kunal came up with, 'Can we see them?' The dexterity with which the man whipped out each pistol made Karl calculate that he must have shot them a minimum of 300 times. And at least 50 per cent of the time he must have shot people. In a heartbeat, Karl concluded that the big gruff gun peddler had shot 150 people. Not knowing if the guns were loaded or not, Kunal started doing what he always did in response to pressure—sweating profusely. The gruff voice added, 'That's a Luger, this here's an old-fashioned Smith & Wesson, this smaller guy is a Berretta.' By now, Kunal had lost his faculty of understanding and the gruff man may as well have introduced the weapons as Aarti, Trupti, Pearl, and Kannan. 'So which one is it? Which one do you want?' Till today, Karl cannot quite explain what happened next. Trying desperately not to displease the tough, he came up with, 'You don't happen to have a water pistol, do you?' When he heard himself say that, Karl thought it was definitely the end of his acting career, the end of their lives, and, worse still, the end of New York for the both of them. However, instead of shooting the two for wasting his time, the big gruff voice began to cry. Yes, he was crying. Crying because he was laughing so hysterically, his tear ducts were activated. He wept and in a choked, stifled voice, kept repeating, 'You don't happen to have a water pistol?'

Days later, when they passed the park again, the large gruff man was there and one look at Karl was enough to send him into convulsions once more. Just like Wild Bill Hickok, John Wesley Hardin, and Jesse

James, another legend had been born on the streets of America. The legend of Water Pistol Karl!

Foreign students largely suffered only one real problem in New York—money. The lack of funds meant that a few rules had to be observed while having a good time.

So far, no American girls had molested either of the boys. Every day that passed seemed to nip that notion further in the bud. The boys decided to take matters into their own hands by visiting one of America's bastions of modern culture, a strip club. After dong their research, the boys found that if four of them went together, they could split the cost of one female stripper.

The girl who came to their table went by the imaginative name of Dr Do. She walked up dressed in her doctor's outfit with a stethoscope and not much else. Dr Do had the bored routine look on her face that one normally sees on people with a government job, which, in all probability, her job was. As she unbuttoned her overloaded shirt, her breasts popped out. It appeared almost accidental. Yaani tried to help her put them back. She then straddled Kunal and continued her strange dance with the same zombie-like expression that a school kid would have developed by the seventh period of the day. A mortified Kunal dared not make eye contact with her pendulous breasts, which were 1 inch and 1½ inches away from his face respectively. Aadith, who normally encountered worse situations at work almost every day, seemed least interested, and so it surprised everyone when his hand sort of wandered out on its own and attacked Dr Do's chest. The good doctor let out a shrill cry that may have included the phrase, 'You damn pervert!' A surprising personal attack on Aadith that begged the question of whether he was a 'damn pervert'. What would she call the rest of the customers? Good Samaritans? Volunteers from the Red Cross? Honours students of Human Biology class?

The boys learnt quickly that the punishment for any physical contact in a 'girlie' bar was swift and absolute. It is one thing to be expelled and debarred from an elite school or college or country club, but to be booted out of a strip club? That placed you on the lowest rung of society right away.

As they perfected the art of acting, not to mention yoga, screenplay writing, and a course in filmmaking, our two Joes also pursued another fine art—the art of binge drinking. Binge drinking could be traced to its founder Jacques-Jean Binge, a lieutenant in Napoleon's army who pioneered the style to get over all his military blunders. Binge was blunder personified. In fact, Napoleon's two big military losses were caused due to him. In the first instance, he led two French battalions to the wrong battlefield, thus allowing the Duke of Wellington to indulge in a bit of French Pummelling. In the second instance, when during the Battle of Trafalgar, victory could have gone either way, he burnt Napoleon's lucky white tights in a fit of incensed ironing. Consequently, Napoleon never appeared in public waist down ever again, and Horatio Nelson heroically carried both the day and Napoleon's sundered tights, which he continually displayed at cocktail parties all over Western Europe until finally an offended member of the royalty ordered that the tights never be seen in public again, as they misrepresented the exact physical proportions of the average French male.

To distract himself from his troubles, Binge (pronounced 'Binjey' until the Americans abbreviated it to 'Binge') would then drink himself silly every evening, thus giving birth to a phrase, which is unpronounceable in French, but which we call 'binge drinking' today.

As the bars were too expensive, the boys went to a supermarket every Friday and bought a six-pack each of the cheapest beer available. This was done after painstaking price comparisons. Invariably, Coor's Lite (which sold for as low as $1.99) won out. The Korean guy who ran the shop never asked them for identification, primarily because he couldn't have been over seventeen himself, and on the odd occasion when the boys ran into his grandfather, the matter solved itself as the old man could never quite pronounce the words 'ID card' properly, and generally gave up after three feeble attempts.

Korean man: You ha IP kaar?

Boys: Pardon?

Korean man: You ha IP kaar?

Boys: Sorry, er what?

Korean man: Never mind, 1 dollar 99.

Boys: Er sorry, what?

Korean man: Silly boy, you no speak English, so why come 'merica'?

The boys would then spend the evening drinking their beers and wandering the streets of Manhattan. Sitting outside the Rockefeller Center or the World Trade Center or on the outskirts of Central Park, they'd soak in the city and get absolutely soaked in turn. Since their energy and enthusiasm wasn't really helping them with the ladies, they decided to focus them towards other goals.

The boys soon began to build a collection of traffic cones. These triangular plastic cones dotted the city's landscape, mostly to indicate a diversion or some unchartable territory, and the boys took it upon themselves to rid the city of them. At one point, they had seventeen such cones lying in their apartment, and only an offer from the building super ('Either the cones stay or you stay') made them donate the cones back to the city.

Lee Strasburg had another bulletin board, which advertised available openings for professional acting work. The roles were chiefly small ones, for Off Broadway productions, but occasionally for film and TV as well. Since there wasn't much available in terms of Indian ethnic characters, the two boys tried their hand at everything. So it was not unusual to see Karl auditioning for the role of a Polish belly dancer, a Greek tycoon's son, even a Norwegian herdsman. Kunal went one step further—he landed a part in a small film called *Hercules in New York*. In it, he was part of a Hispanic chain gang that attacks Hercules in Central Park. It was a great coup as his was a speaking part. His exact words were, 'Kill him,' or rather 'Keeel heeem,' followed by an 'Aaah...' or more likely an 'Arghhhh' as Hercules unceremoniously flings Kunal twenty feet across the lawn into Central Park. The good news was that Kunal was great in the part. The bad news—the shot required nine takes.

Of course, Karl accompanied Kunal for the audition and insisted on playing the role of manager. The interaction between the Polish American film director, Paul Bruzinski, and Karl went something like this.

Karl: Hi, I'm Kunal's manager.

Director: What's a Kunal?

Karl: He's one of the lead actors in the scene in which the Hispanic gang attacks Hercules in the park.

Director: Hmm.

Karl: Well, nobody's given Kunal his lines.

Director: Who gives a fuck?

Karl: 'Who gives a fuck?' Are those his lines?

Director: Fuck off.

Karl: Who gives a fuck. Fuck off. Okay. Anything else?

Director: Fuck you.

Karl: Who gives a fuck, fuck off, fuck you. Er... anything else?

Director: Fuck you again.

Karl: Okay, that's quite a bit. Hang on, let me get a piece of paper.

Kunal received the princely sum of $200 for his effort, although they were both perplexed by the production person's farewell remark, 'Make sure I never see you again.' Anyway, it's very difficult to decipher what Americans mean. They twist the English language until it makes about as much sense as Japanese to an Indian ear.

Hercules in New York was not given the kind of grand opening Kunal and Karl had hoped for. It didn't open at the famous Chinese theatre in LA. In fact, it opened and apparently shut down in some obscure

Bulgarian student film festival. Kunal remained optimistic: maybe, one day his true worth would be recognized and he'd become Bulgaria's biggest superstar. He began his preparation for this momentous occasion by asking his friend an important question, 'What's the capital of Bulgaria?' Little did he know what fate had in store for him...and for Bulgaria.

Enter Khalid Jani. The boys had about two weeks to go on the course when they found a strange note on the bulletin board: 'Need 5 male and 2 female actors for "magnimental" production in Hindi languages. Indian/Pakistani type best admired.' It was signed by a man who called himself 'Noted actor, producer, writer, choreographer, director, man in a million, one amongst only one, Khalid Jani.' The ad then listed all the awards won by Khalid Jani, totalling 27. They included the illustrious 'Mahila Mandal of Matunga North East Award for Excellence', 'The Dinesh Kulkarni Scholarship for Champion 100 m Sprinter in the Under Fifteen Category', and the 'Best Show Dog for Bonnie in the Toy Dog Category'.

Khalid Jani's ad quickly left its imprint. The students took turns correcting the English. India and Indians suddenly became very popular. Students would sporadically break into fake Indian accents, confusing singulars and plurals. 'All actor, come to assembly halls now', or 'How many person to act in play?' Karl and Kunal had to endure some extended leg-pulling, but remained unperturbed. They could hear destiny calling, albeit in incorrect English and with a host of inappropriate awards. They decided to go and meet 'India's Jewel from Kohinoor Fame, one and only one, Khalid Jani'.

123

And then they met him. New York City will always be a leading centre for fashion. Trends, styles, both conventional and offbeat, will always come out of the Big Apple, but even New York was not prepared for what was to hit her next. Of the millions who walked her streets day after day, wearing things as varied as Chinese silks and Maldivian wools, lycra and fake leather, nothing, no, nothing came close to the iconic fashion sense of Khalid Jani. Khalid Jani was from a northern state in India, and came to Mumbai at the age of eighteen in order to become the next Amitabh Bachchan. In fact, throughout his limited schooling, when asked about his proposed occupation, he would say firmly: 'To be the next Amitabh Bachchan.' Even in his younger days, he promoted his original sartorial style. This was done through deft little touches, like a feather tucked behind his ear or a flower in his hair.

When Khalid Jani entered Strasburg, word got out quickly and soon the whole school had gathered to take a look at this exotic being. Khalid Jani was dressed in sky blue from head to toe. He had on what could best be described as a blue jacket over blue bottoms with blue pointed shoes that were only worn by clowns and villains in cartoon films. On his head was a blue bandana and an extra large pair of blue sunglasses. To add a splash of colour, a bright yellow belt hung from his ample waist. His jacket was worn open, allowing a generous glimpse of a thicket of black hair. His pointed shoes had four-inch heels on them that clearly seemed to say that Khalid Jani couldn't be any taller than a footstool. He had rings and bells on his fingers, and about 37 different types of necklaces hung around his neck. One could also see from his face that Khalid Jani was disappointed. Disappointed that having come to a meeting ground of fellow artists and thespians, he found them all to be dressed quite simply and none, not one, like himself. Khalid Jani was a promoter of the 'one colour' idea—one colour from head to toe. This is why he felt people in the army or the police always seemed the best dressed.

Jani was provided a room in Strasburg to conduct his auditions or, as he put it, 'additions'. He was stunned at the response to his ad. A total of 213 students auditioned for his upcoming project. Most of them were Caucasians, although a few African Americans and Chinese Americans also took a shot at it. Nobody wanted to act in his project but everyone wanted an experience they could narrate to their grandchildren after years of therapy. Only two of the 213 were actually of Indian stock, two young men named Karl and Kunal.

Jani's movie was about a group of villagers in Haryana who challenge bullying British soldiers to a game of cricket (which the villagers had never played before) to settle their disputes. After many months of researching and searching, Jani zeroed in on his British soldiers: a group of seven European tourists he found at Café Leopold, Mumbai. The seven, mostly from Belgium, were down for three months, which was just about time enough for him to complete his task. On screen, the seven would function as eleven, with four doubling up in certain scenes in which they would use their moustaches to distinguish themselves from well… er, themselves. With the soldiers cast, he turned his attention to the Indian cast.

Khalid Jani's last film called *Aakhree Phonecall* (*Last Phonecall*) was doing the rounds of various film festivals. It had been to Venice, France, Germany, Greece, and was now competing for Sundance. The film's theme was a man who could make phone calls by using only his mind, which led to mayhem and the huge problem of how to bill him. Wherever Khalid journeyed, he'd audition Indians for his film. He firmly believed that Indians abroad made for better Indians. The audition, largely in Hindi, soon became farcical as all the non-Indians would come and do bad Indian accents, mostly doing impressions of Khalid himself, and then leave laughing hysterically. Khalid was disappointed. He felt Strasburg's acting standards weren't up to scratch. After auditioning 200 non-Indians who had been asked to make animal sounds, Khalid was pretty certain that Karl and Kunal were the two actors for him. To see how good they were at their craft, he didn't bother them with a long audition but just asked them one important question.

Khalid Jani: Have you seen my last picture?

Karl and Kunal: Yes.

Khalid Jani: What is its name?

Karl and Kunal: *Aakhree Phonecall*.

Khalid immediately recognized their talent and signed them on for his new project, tentatively titled *The Gaonwallah, The Britisher, and The Ugly*. This was later to be shortened to *Aatma Kee Keemath* (*The Price of the Soul*). For all his blue finery, Khalid already had written contracts, names were filled in, English corrected, and the contracts handed over. Kunal and Karl were ecstatic. Yes, he may have been the man who made *Aakhree Phonecall*, he may have been the man who made *Nabbey se Ninyanwey* (*Ninety to Ninety-nine*), he may have been the man whose first film was the epitome of surreal sleaze (a new film genre, by the way) titled *Neela Blouse* (*The Blue Blouse*), but a movie is a movie, and they had come to be actors, wanted to be actors, and you can't really call yourself an actor until you've actually done a film, no matter that the film may be called *The Gaonwallah, The Britisher, and The Ugly* (tentative title).

Typically, in Indian 'filmi' lore, when a newcomer is given his first break, he is paid only a token amount of money for his efforts. Karl and Kunal were to be launched in Khalid's film, albeit with 27 other lead characters, and so the money offered wasn't great—approximately 10,000 rupees each. Yet, this was more money than they were used to. Theatre, radio, and voiceovers didn't exactly turn you into a Rockefeller overnight.

That very evening, they were invited for a tête-à-tête with Khalid Jani in his hotel room in Queens. True to form, Khalid Jani was in a maroon blazer with matching pants and boots. He had on a top hat, which he'd clearly stolen from an out-of-work ringmaster. He sat on an orange couch, and next to him sat 'Breast Personified', or more likely, 'Breast Womanohed'. She was a pair of huge breasts imported from Sweden to which was loosely attached a little face and perhaps a pair of legs, though neither Karl nor Kunal bothered to look low enough; they were quite satisfied with the panoramic view above, thank you very much.

Khalid Jani, who by now had graduated to wearing actual carpets (he had on a yellow rug that may earlier have been used as a bathmat), unzipped his jacket to exactly three inches below his navel and tried to match breasts with Inge. This was an obviously futile attempt to draw attention back to himself, and on 99 occasions out of 100, a man wearing a bathmat unzipped to well below his navel would have been the cynosure of all eyes. But even a colourful personality like Khalid was outdone by Breast Woman.

'Thee pictures start with thee camera panning to thee boy's foot, it is bleeding. Stop. Pan to other foot, it is not bleeding. Pan to one arm, it is bleeding. Stop. Pan to other arm, it is not bleeding. By nows, all the peoples or asking kee whats will happen next? This is always my keys to films by Khalid Jani. In thee very first scene, in thee very first shot I likes to grab the person by the ball.'

He then went on to add, 'All the bleedings were caused by the British, and all the healings must be caused by the Indians themselves.' That was the one-line story of the film. He nodded and waited for the boys to respond. Obviously, the boys hadn't heard a word, being very busy with their empirical research on female secondary sexual organs.

Khalid Jani convinced the boys to finish their course as quickly as possible as he wanted to 'commence shooting' in the next 45 days. Thus, the boys had to squeeze their classes and work harder on weekends in order to get done a little earlier.

chapter 6

After three months away, the boys were back in Mumbai. They felt they had returned as conquering heroes. Sadly, there was no ticker tape parade; in fact, it seemed as if no one had noticed their absence. The only person who seemed interested in contacting them was Khalid Jani's right hand and third cousin, Illyas, who was twice removed and then reinstated.

The two boys tried telling their respective fathers of their break into Bollywood. Let's start with Karl and Jehaan. Karl approached his father when he was at his most approachable, early in the morning.

Karl: Dad, by the way, I've got a prominent role in Khalid Jani's new blockbuster, *The Gaonwallah, The Britisher, and The Ugly*.

Jehaan: Did you leave the pot seat up in our bathroom? Your mother's going nuts thinking it's me. However, you tell me honestly, three months this doesn't happen, now you return...and on the first day the pot seat is up!

Karl: Dad, did you hear what I said? This is a major break. A Khalid Jani film, *The Gaonwallah, The Britisher, and The Ugly*. Kunal's also in it.

Jehaan: I see, so who's going to play the other two roles, The Gaonwallah and The Britisher?

Kunal fared slightly better. As Kunal's dad suffered from chronic backache, the best time to engage him in a conversation was when he was writhing and squirming on his back.

Kunal: Dad, I've got a good role in a Khalid Jani film.

Kunal's Dad: Aah, aah, ugh.

Kunal: It's called *The Gaonwallah, The Britisher, and The Ugly.*

Kunal's Dad: Make sure you are playing... aah... ouch... aha... aha... the Britisher.

Disappointed by the lack of enthusiasm shown by friends and family, the two boys were soon caught in the whirlpool of pre-production activity for the film. At the very outset, they were introduced to one of Bollywood's legendary characters, The Tailor. The Tailor went by the highly respected title of 'Masterji'. This is like addressing your building manager with the title 'Your Eminence'. Masterji's headquarters were a hole in the wall in Colaba. Masterji himself was 10,500 years old, completely blind, and worse still, clearly suffering from Parkinson's. This made his efforts with a measuring tape quite an uphill task. Karl and Kunal soon came to understand the peculiar working habits of the filmi tailor.

Masterji started measuring the body parts shoulder downwards, at the speed of a dying ember. This was okay on the shoulders but definitely a no-no on the inner thighs. As Masterji's old, wiry, bony fingers wrapped around his thigh, Karl started grunting like a pig. Oblivious to Karl's awkwardness, Masterji proceeded even more slowly, and a half hour later, he finally wound the tape around Karl's thigh, only to break suddenly into conversation with his junior staff about some heroine's unfinished choli. Meanwhile, a wiser Kunal started taking his own measurements and writing them down. When it was actually his turn, he offered the measurements to Masterji. At this point, Karl and Kunal were made privy to a truly life-altering miracle. The blind 10,500-year-old, Parkinson-ridden dying ember of a tailor sprang to life like the steroid-pumped Ben Johnson. Screaming himself hoarse, he tore Kunal's paper to shreds. He then began flinging things at Kunal—first the torn pieces of paper, then the tape, then his slippers, and then a steel mug. By the time he flung the iron, the boys had done a little Ben Johnson act of their own. Masterji came screaming down the alley behind them with a pantsuit and a hanger dangling from his extended arms, to be used as weapons to subdue Kunal.

It took thousands of phone calls and messages to soothe Masterji's bruised ego, and effect some sort of reconciliation. Even so, he refused to measure Kunal himself, and asked one of his lowly female assistants to do the needful. That day, the boys learnt a very important lesson about the hierarchy in tinsel town. The character actor was at the bottom, the director one step above, then came the hero, and finally the producer occupied the highest position. Yet, above all of them was a two-bit untalented tailor known as 'Masterji'.

Next on the boys' agenda was what separated the men from the boys. This was what made an actor, and made a person a screen legend—dance rehearsals. The latter are unique to the Indian film industry. Often films enter production with unfinished scripts and plots, not all the actors may have been signed on, finances may not be available, and technicians and locations may remain undecided; but what shines bright and constant through the chaos is the dance rehearsal. Every Indian actor, young or old, male or female, gifted or otherwise, has had to undergo the grind of dance rehearsals. Also, this is one aspect of the film that never seems to be affected by budgets: all films have a dance routine, in a big budget film the heroine wears fewer clothes, in a small budget film *everyone* wears fewer clothes.

Karl and Kunal hadn't much idea about the plot of the movie, no clue about their characters, or any news about the rest of the cast. All they knew was that they had been fitted for costumes and that their attendance at dance rehearsals was compulsory. There was only one problem. The rehearsals were in Andheri, and Andheri, as Pink Floyd once pointed out, was on the dark side of the moon. Living as they did in south Mumbai, close to the Colaba tip, while Andheri was in the north and much nearer Scotland, the two boys found themselves in a quandary.

Karl: Five days in a row to Andheri and back will kill us.

Kunal: We'll need five more days just to recover.

Karl: Forget the damn dance rehearsals, what if they shoot the whole film in Andheri?

Kunal: You think we can return the money?

Karl: (Expletive that rhymes with an edible water bird) No amount of money can compensate us for travelling to Andheri and back.

Kunal: I'd rather go to hell, man!

Karl: Yes, it'll be much shorter!

Filled with misgivings and dread, the boys started on their long journey.

Yogesh Shetty had two things going for him; he was an extremely athletic and gifted dancer/choreographer, and was already an established name in Bollywood with dance classes all over the city. He was also the man with the smallest waist in the world.

Karl: It couldn't be more than four inches.

Kunal: His belt is exactly half the size of my shoelace.

Yogesh Shetty was very articulate, well mannered, and extremely effete. Rumour had it, though it was difficult to authenticate, that Yogesh was a practising man lover. Seated by his side at all times was a young, rough, hirsute lad called Dipesh. Dipesh, whose bloodline included the British Bulldog, had a muscular frame and a pug-like face. When Yogesh spoke to Dipesh, he always addressed him as 'Dipooo'.

Yogesh: What are your names?

Karl: I'm Karl. The good-looking one is Kunal.

Yogesh: Whatever, have you ever danced before?

Karl: No.

Kunal: Thousands of times.

Karl: Did you say thousands of times?

Kunal: Yeah, you know, at birthday parties, weddings, sangeets, navjots…er, building events.

Karl (interrupting): You idiot, that's not what he means…

Karl started whacking the back of Kunal's head like a woodpecker to a tree trunk.

Kunal: It's hurting…just stop.

Yogesh: Dipooo! Who are these jokers? Why are they here? Are we making an animal picture? I mean even I can't teach bears to dance. I'm only human, there's only so much I can do. Why can't they ever, ever, ever send me someone who can actually DANCE?

Dipooo: Huh!

Dipooo immediately did what he always did. He led the newcomers away from Yogesh to the safe confines of a dark corner, and started working on them with a little less emotion than Arnold Schwarzenegger showed in *Terminator*. For the next six hours, the boys underwent their first filmi dance rehearsal. It was far worse than theatre. Six hours were spent dancing to just four lines. The English translation of the couplet went roughly like this:

Your cheeks are extremely white/pale,

Your jaw is extremely soft/stale,

Your hair is falling, may I pat it back?

Your hands are so pure, may I get a slap?

Hour after hour of dancing to the same line can break down a hardened criminal, as evidenced by the work of the Mossad in the Yom Kippur War. Karl and Kunal came away broken.

Karl: What the hell have we done?

Kunal: It must be punishment, penance for our sins.

Karl: Exactly my point, what the hell have we done?

How they got through those initial rehearsals is a question only their diaries and spurious drugs may reveal.

The next month found them in New Delhi to shoot the first part of the film *The Gaonwallah, The Britisher, and The Ugly*…er, that's still a tentative title.

Since the boys weren't stars, they were put up in a guesthouse called Sherwani. Delhi is riddled with guesthouses, most of them built over 700 years ago during the days of the Tughlaq dynasty. These guesthouses have a unique feature—they either have electricity or water but never both. Sherwani, however, was a more upmarket guesthouse. The boys' room had an air-conditioner. Unfortunately, just above the AC was a large window without a pane. Thus exposed to the elements, the AC was for all practical purposes, completely redundant. Sherwani's most promising feature was its menu card. Nine dishes were mentioned on the menu; and next to seven, the bold letters 'NA' were marked. This stood for 'Not Available'. The two dishes that were available were yellow dal and white rice. But again, the letters 'CWK' (Check with Kitchen) were prominently placed beside those.

Karl and Kunal thought Delhi was absurd. First, the sing-song rhythm when people spoke took some getting used to. Then, the third word of every sentence had to be rhymed nonsensically. For instance, a Delhiite would say, 'Are you hungry-shungry? Want some food-shood? Let's go to hotel-shotel for some khana-wana.' The boys found the next feature both peculiar and disturbing. 'Proximity violation', that is, violation of personal space, was always a huge irritant for both Karl and Kunal. Unfortunately, in New Delhi, creating and maintaining a personal space was generally thought unacceptable. None proved this better than the fourth assistant director, a sixteen-year-old boy called Vikramjeet.

The first day of the shoot was outside the famous Qutub Minar garden.

Vikramjeet: You boys have to walk-shalk from the rock-cock to here. Don't look at each other-shutter, walk like normal-shormal. Got it?

Kunal: Got it…er, one thing…

Vikramjeet: Haah. Bolo, tell me.

Kunal: Can you let go of my hand?

The boys had an amazing first day. All the secondary characters had a couple of shots each. Karl and Kunal had to do a brief walk, after which they got a five-hour break. This was followed by a second shot in which Kunal's character, Gagan, got to say a line to Karl's character, predictably called Magan.

Gagan: Arrey yaar. (Pushes)

Magan: Aahhah!! (Falls)

Why did their characters behave in this way? Who were they? Why were they called Gagan and Magan? These questions were met with the same answer from Vikramjeet—Khalid says everything will become clear-shear when you see the movie…twice.

In Indian society, a leading film hero's position is just above God's. The whole of Delhi will attend a film shoot to try and see the hero, or God, or both, preferably sans make-up. It is also interesting to note that nowhere else in the world is a film hero known as 'hero'. For example, in America, Sylvester Stallone is commonly known as Sylvester Stallone. On the film set, a typical conversation between spectators would go like this:

'When is the hero coming?'

'He's arrived, he's on the set.'

'He's arrived. I better tell everyone. Everyone, the hero has come. Everyone, the hero has come.'

This last line is then repeated 344 times till the entire city of Delhi, nay, the whole of the tri-state area, nay, the whole of India, is completely aware that the hero has indeed arrived and will shortly do something heroic, like a dance sequence involving two somersaults, one backward and one forward.

The unit had been shooting for roughly two weeks before the hero arrived. His name was Yusuf Khan. He was one of the biggest stars in the country although physically he was one of the smallest. Yusuf was known as the King of the College Romance. This sobriquet was fine for the first nineteen years of his career, but now at 46 years of age, it was getting more and more difficult to convince people. In fact, in his last two movies, screenwriters had gone to great pains to have his character mention repeatedly that he was in his last year of college and clearly a senior.

The last two years had been hell for Yusuf personally. He'd had three hair transplants, the last of which was the most humiliating as hair from his ears was transplanted on to his head. His tummy tuck had not gone unnoticed, and that blasted *Cine-High* magazine had broken a story on the inner shoe heels he wore, thus challenging his stated height of five feet three inches. *Cine-High* put it at five feet one inch at best, and gave irrefutable evidence that Yusuf Khan never acted with a child in the same frame, in a clear bid not to expose his height or rather the lack of it.

Yusuf was also very fond of rings and chains. He wore no less than 33 bracelets, rings, and trinkets. It didn't matter if his character was a rich brat or an absolute pauper, the bling remained the same. Yusuf also insisted that in all his films, his character must be called Rohit. Things came to a head when he had to play the title role in *Ali Baba and the Forty Thieves*. Finally, a compromise was reached. Rohit was used as the character's first name and Ali Baba made up the surname.

Yusuf had another demand. He had to be allowed to sing at least one song in every film. This was fine except for the fact that Rohit had a terrible voice. Behind his back, producers called him the man with the voice of a dying donkey.

On the day of Yusuf's arrival in Delhi, Karl and Kunal were invited to his trailer for a briefing. As they entered the huge trailer, they bumped into a giant egg, which turned out to be Yusuf's head. Obviously, the transplants hadn't been too effective, and to keep up with the character—a 23-year-old called Rohit— Yusuf had been compelled to wear a wig. A wig that he thought had come from the famous British wig makers Haig and Beacon, but had actually been pilfered from his heroine Sujatha's mother by Yusuf's cunning make-up man, Shirishbhai. So eventually *The Gaonwallah, The Britisher, and The Ugly* would star Sujatha in the female lead, and someone who looked exactly like Sujatha's mother, only perhaps shorter, in the male lead.

Interestingly, Yusuf took an instant liking to Kunal and Karl. He insisted they spend all their free time in his trailer. Yusuf discriminated among the other character actors on grounds of class. Karl and Kunal were different. Yusuf missed people from his own background and adopted the boys immediately.

Now, the moment a leading hero adopts you, your status changes. You become the most important and wanted member of the production. Since you have the King's ear, you are the glue that can bind all disparate elements into a successful shooting schedule.

As they grew closer to Yusuf, Karl and Kunal were slightly corrupted by their sense of power. They might hint to Yusuf that today was not a great day to work and should instead be used for some active rest and recreation. The shoot would then be unceremoniously cancelled, leaving Jani exasperated. Then Yusuf, Sujatha, Karl, and Kunal would go over to Yusuf's hotel where they'd all play games like dumb charades, during the course of which Karl and Kunal were convinced that Yusuf was a terrible actor and that Sujatha was actually worse.

Yusuf was working on seventeen different films simultaneously. He couldn't remember most of the titles, but he did know his character's name in each ...Rohit. The King of the College Romance now decided to push his two friends into some of these films. When he asked the producer of 7 *Ladies* (in which an all-female cast supported Yusuf) to create roles for Karl and Kunal in that film, he met with some resistance.

Producer: But Yusuf sir, the whole idea is to have you as the only male character, surrounded by females.

It is every man's fantasy, first time in India. I can't put these two boys anywhere. You see, we've already cast for the waiters, drivers, and dead bodies.

Yusuf: See Pandey, you always see problems. There are no problems, only solutions. You say all-girl cast? You don't want any males, right?

Producer: Yes sir, I've even got permission from my wife to make this film. Only females. Only females. It's the greatest idea in cinema.

Yusuf: Okay, then Karl and Kunal will play females. Change the title to *9 Ladies*, okay?

Producer: Er…er, *9 Ladies*…er, *Plus Two*?

And so Karl and Kunal were suddenly making appearances in eight different productions, and in one of them they would debut as part of an all-female cast!

The films had interesting names, ranging from the *Curse of the Black Python* to *Marine Drive* to *Chinghiz Khan*. The last was a biopic of the life of Chinghiz Khan, with Yusuf in the lead. The only problem of course was Yusuf's insistence that Chinghiz Khan's character be given the pet name 'Rohit', which historian/director Saeed Ali would not allow under any circumstances. Saeed Ali already had allowed two pivotal roles to go to two unknown boys. Now to allow history's greatest conqueror to answer occasionally to the name 'Rohit' was utterly preposterous. Saeed Ali's artistic temperament was about to snap. When Yusuf said he'd confine the use of 'Rohit' to the love scenes, Saeed snapped, 'What love scenes? There are rapes, which I will show in their stark brutality. During one of these rapes, if you

140

like, I'll send your boys in with the line, "Excuse me, Rohit, there's a phone call for you"!'

Yusuf was a sensitive man, and was hurt by Ali's sarcasm. Saeed Ali eventually had his way, but only on condition that the credits would read 'Chinghiz Khan/Rohit—Yusuf Khan'.

chapter 7

Karl and Kunal had eight projects in hand, none of which were complete, and had also pocketed a sizeable sum in 'signing amounts'. A doctor or a lawyer spends years building a successful practice and a reputation. An actor on the other hand joins the big league in a matter of minutes. Without a single release, Karl and Kunal started seeing their names in film glossies, newspapers, tabloids, and other milestones of modern-day literature.

But Karl and Kunal really outdid themselves where all actors ultimately aspire to be—filmi parties. Two incidents elevated their status overnight, and both occurred at the same party.

Yusuf Khan called the boys and asked them to attend his costume party. It was after all his thirty-seventh birthday (and in all probability the last of the ten times he'd be celebrating it), and a fancy dress party would set the pace. The party was in the suburbs of Mumbai where Yusuf had a three-storeyed bungalow called Ocean View. Ocean View was inappropriately named as there wasn't an ocean in sight, and it also became the 314th property in Mumbai with that name. In fact, 74 per cent of all Mumbai's buildings and bungalows share just four names: (a) Ocean View, (b) Sea View, (c) Garden View, and (d) Park View.

Yusuf Khan and his wife Celina greeted all the guests at the front door. Yusuf was dressed as a giant crab, which guests mistook for his mother-in-law. In fact, he had tried to disguise himself as the action hero of yesteryears, Vishwas, who was known for his roles as a medieval knight in a suit of armour that was rarely cleaned. Celina, who hated these parties, was dressed as Celina. Behind her back, sniggers could be heard about how being herself simply meant dressing like a witch. Thanks to her snooty disposition, unfriendly demeanour, and sharp tongue, Celina usually got strangers to dislike her within the first few seconds of interaction.

Karl and Kunal debated long and hard about what to wear to fit in. Karl decided to dress up as the Pink Panther; however, due to an unforeseen incident with the tailor, he had to make do with a maroon felt suit that made him resemble a three-month pregnant weasel, rather than a sleek panther. Kunal, always the more adventurous of the two, decided to dress as his favourite fruit, the watermelon. Here again the tailor forgot to make any outlets for his legs, so Karl literally had to roll Kunal along at a slow pace, which made for a happy watermelon, but an unhappy Kunal. As they entered the party, Kunal said, 'Whatever you do, don't leave me, I can't roll on my own.' And after a moment, 'Oh God, Karl, hell, we forgot!'

Karl: Forgot what?

Kunal: What if I need to go to the toilet?

Film stars, models, actors, wannabes, technicians,

businessmen, lowlifers, furry animals—they were all there. The party was grand. In true filmi style, lots of men were dancing with other men, oblivious to all the cleavage generously on display. Kunal, who was having great trouble stuffing a cheese sandwich into the little cloth opening that was shared by his eyes, nose, and mouth, suddenly found himself in the centre of the Mumbai salsa. As the dance increased in vigour, a new element was introduced. As you circled the watermelon, you had to plant a kick on its behind. Now any watermelon specialist will tell you that no watermelon worth its melon actually has a behind. This resulted in people aiming kicks at different reference points on Kunal's...er, body. He got kicked in the stomach, chest, abdomen, hamstring, kneecap, and even once in the head. The whirring dervishes just kept getting faster and faster, with heightened screams, until suddenly the veteran actor OP Kumar fell dead. He had tried to join the fun but the exertion proved too much for the unfortunate 79-year-old. He planted a kick on the watermelon's knee and both he and the watermelon collapsed on the floor. Initially, neither got up. This was probably because twelve pairs of feet were stamping on them simultaneously. Finally, a few people pulled Kunal up by the string on his head mask. OP Kumar, however, remained comatose.

The next day, newspapers cried out headlines such as 'Legendary Actor Felled by Watermelon', 'Veteran Vegetarian Thespian Murdered by a Fruit', 'Forget About an Apple a Day, a Melon One Day Killed OP Kumar'. Thereafter, Kunal became a household name.

'Did he hate OP Kumar?', 'Had he killed anybody else before, disguised as a fruit?', 'Did OP Kumar make a pass at him?', 'Did OP Kumar have a history with watermelons?'

Kunal's parents were quite distraught. They didn't know which was worse, that their son may have killed OP Kumar or that he had done it disguised as a watermelon.

The papers were also filled with another story.

In the middle of the party, Karl had stumbled upon a woman wearing a Wonder Woman mask and a full coat that threatened to expose her Wonder Woman figure. The woman seemed quite fascinated by the young man who proceeded to teach her one of the most advanced of dance steps—the Karl Shuffle. This dance evolved from the need to rest one's arms and legs and yet convey the idea that one was involved in a frantic new modern dance interpretation. It was achieved by simply slamming your chin into your chest and then back up again. This simple bobbing of the head coupled with poor lighting at parties produced the illusion that the dancer involved was dancing out of his shoes when nothing could be further from the truth. Wonder Woman seemed charmed by the Karl Shuffle or the chin step. Just after the watermelon incident, the couple found themselves in a dark corner of the hall. Unfortunately, it wasn't dark enough. Wonder Woman embraced Karl and then proceeded to unbutton her coat and simultaneously slip off her mask. She needn't have bothered. What met Karl's eyes made him tremble with fear, a fear he hadn't felt since the first time he had heard his father sing. A skin that would have suited a Tyrannosaurus Rex more was exposed. Wonder Woman was old. During practice, as a young boy, he had run the 50 metres in under six seconds, but this wasn't practice, this was the very Olympic final itself. He broke all national records on his way out.

The next day, the papers were filled with stories of how the Grand Old Lady of Bollywood, Romaana (also known as Battle Barracuda), had claimed her next victim. The old lady was well known for her age and her penchant for young boys. As she aged, her hunger for boys grew. Karl was one in a long line of victims, and he was not to be the last either, but he wished fervently that he had had a protective watermelon armour on, like his prudent friend Kunal.

Romaana hadn't acted in a film in 45 years. She lived like a recluse in a large suburban bungalow. But like all barracudas young or old, she needed to be fed sooner or later. That was when she'd turn up at one of the better parties to source her prey. Once her prey was in sight, she became absolutely obsessed, and would go to any lengths to track him down. For the next few days, Karl lived in great fear. First she caught him outside a crowded bus stop and proceeded to make a scene.

Romaana: I love you, I love you, why are you treating me so badly? Why are you hiding your feelings?

By now, Karl was hiding much more than his feelings, he was hiding himself. He did this by entering a moving bus and then exiting from it a few metres away, then without turning back, he ran like the wind. Mrs Barracuda then stationed herself outside his building, at the swimming pool, and even in a male urinal. Finally, desperate and frightened, he turned to Yusuf Khan.

Yusuf: See, I'll tell you, we've all experienced it. The only thing to do is bite the bullet. Once she's satisfied, she won't bother you again. Think of her as the Black Widow spider that never mates with the same spider more than once.

Karl: She never mates again. Why?

Yusuf: After the act, she eats her mate alive.

Karl felt like a limp biscuit by the time the Battle Barracuda was done with him. They were the worst moments of his life thus far. But he rose to the occasion after much initial difficulty. At first, the troops refused to come out and the soldiers failed to make a formation; and then they refused to fire. Karl made a brave speech to his men, telling them that if they could perform today for queen and country, he would never ask anything of them again. He then remembered how Babar in a drunken fit swore to give up drink in an effort to inspire his men. Karl too had to give up something he loved. He toyed with haircuts, wearing shorts, and Kunal. But better sense prevailed. Haircuts and shorts were far too important, so he swore to his men that they'd seen the last of Kunal, and if they could just play a final overture, they'd never see the Battle Barracuda again. It is said that in times of extreme danger, one's character is revealed. It was the last time he met or heard from Mrs Brontosaurus. But at what price! People in the know sniggered when he passed. Sick of the watermelon attention, Kunal was relieved that the focus had shifted to Karl.

Kunal: Ay, Karl, next year let's go to France where you can make out with the Eiffel Tower, she's a good four hundred years old too.

Kunal: Let's go to the Hanging Gardens and visit the old woman and the shoe. Oh no, that's right, that would make it twice today, right?

Karl had no recourse but to grin and bear it. In the meantime, Yusuf Khan became a part of their everyday lives. This was chiefly because of a passion they all shared. They liked to play Scrabble.

A loose history of Scrabble is probably required here. Scrabble was invented by the court of Henry IV (Part I), approximately 527 years ago. Henry IV suffered from one of the worst peculiarities an English king could suffer from. He didn't speak a word of English. Not even privately, like all Indians do. After 33½ years of miscommunication, he hired a group of tutors who went by the name *Ballet de Sade*, which is French for 'a group of tutors'. Six months of regular conventional teaching yielded few results. Yes, the King did get 'A'…for 'apple', but he also insisted on 'L' for 'L'apple' and '2' for '2apple', not to mention 'P' for 'pineapple'. Utterly discouraged, the *Ballet de Sade* decided to change their tack. Pushed to the brink, they realized that through a spelling game that the King always would win, slowly but surely they'd obtain positive results. Now, although Henry IV (Part I) never mastered the tongue, he did become the world's first German speller, which is a particularly unusual outcome when you consider that he was a Frenchman trying desperately to learn English.

Yusuf Khan was a lot like Henry IV. His first tongue

was French, and he came to love Scrabble more than life itself. He famously commented that his day was not complete without the five great 'S'es—sleep, sex, Scrabble, a shower, and Cher. It became routine for Karl and Kunal to spend the evening with Yusuf in his house or movie trailer, and unwind with an hour or so of Scrabble.

Yusuf, of course, epitomized the phrase 'to cheat'. He was an out-and-out, complete, and supreme 'fakado' (early Japanese for 'a lying cheat'). He'd invent words without blinking, and would explain them in a convincing, pedagogic tone, e.g. 'The word "swanko", basically means something both swanky and inexpensive, like Aarti's boob job.' Other words that became part of the Yusuf Khan lexicon include Desparadillo: a rodent found in the Savannah, Geryitirim: a sort of plutonium only found on Uranus, Cuppercle: a sort of cuftan worn in East Timor, and Mammolahs: elephant breasts.

The games followed a particular routine. Yusuf would take an early lead, make up word after non-sensical word, and then win the game, leaving the boys marvelling at his vast vocabulary. This went down very well with Yusuf who was made up of 11 per cent muscle, 8 per cent water, and 81 per cent ego. After massacring the young men mercilessly at Scrabble day after day, he decided to repay them for their incompetence. For a long time, Yusuf had toyed with the idea of a three-man, Marx Brothers-type comedy routine. He had a script in place but didn't feel he had a crack team. He then wondered, what if he teamed up with the two boys? As long as their chemistry was a little better than their spelling, they might just have something here.

In a few years' time, Karl and Kunal had appeared in quite a few films. Some released, the better ones didn't. We catch up with them once again at the release of the Yusuf-, Karl-, Kunal starrer called *A Night at a Musical*. Yusuf was very particular about promoting the idea of original scripts and Indian themes in his body of work. This body of work included (1) *Vayu*, based on *Titanic*, (2) *Nashta at Kayani's*, based on *Breakfast at Tiffany's*, and (3) *Rambhaa*, based on *Rambo*, although to be completely fair, *Rambhaa* was based on all four Rambo movies combined.

A Night at a Musical was a scene-by-scene, line-by-line lift of *A Night at the Opera*, made famous by the Marx Brothers. Here, Groucho was played by Yusuf, Chico by Karl, and Harpo by Kunal. Tenor Allan Jones's role was taken on by the almost but not quite soprano voice of Nikhilesh, arguably the most queer singer in the subcontinent.

The highlight of the film is when the three brothers, The Brothers Munshi (Yusuf felt that would throw the original performers off their scent), and 255 people find themselves in a single cabin on board a ship. This beat the Marx Brothers' record of 224 people by a wide margin. Yusuf used this statistic widely in his publicity campaign, but straight-facedly denied being inspired by the Marx Brothers' original in any way. It was most definitely his best piece of acting, both on or off camera.

On opening night, the reviews were very favourable. The actual print reviews were even better. *Mumbai*

Today: 'A complete lift of the original', *Nation's Express*: 'If you grew up after the Marx Brothers and are not conversant in English, this is the film for you', and *The Hindustan Chronicle* said, 'Even for a cheap low borrower of ideas and energy, stealing the cult movie *A Night at the Opera* is an all-time low. So in a sense Yusuf Khan should be proud of how low he's actually stooped this time.'

As with most rip-offs, the movie was a huge hit. Overnight, Karl and Kunal went from being minor celebrities to players in the big league. The team of Yusuf, Karl, and Kunal was here to stay.

Yusuf was so drunk with his success that he started telling everyone that he was getting feelers from Hollywood. Indeed, he did get a feeler in the shape of a show-cause notice from the makers of *A Night at the Opera*. This was to cost him financially later on. But for the moment, Yusuf Khan decided to look at the positive side. Hollywood, yes Hollywood, had contacted him. He instantly made up his new word for the day, a word that meant 'he who was the first to cross over from mainstream Bollywood to mainstream Hollywood'. Yusuf was the first 'Hollywoodstani'.

The Brothers Munshi soon gained a colossal fan following. On a promotional trip to Lucknow, the master of ceremonies introduced them to his audience with these words:

MC: First, we have award-winning actors Kunal and Karl who, after acting in many Hollywood films, have now made Mumbai and India their own. Kunal is also a trained karate master (3rd Dan), and Karl gave up a promising career in medicine to become an actor. In other words, he simply shifted theatres. He gave up the operation theatre for the actual theatre. [Pause for laughter] [No laughter forthcoming] [More awkward pause] And now it gives me great pleasure to introduce the most sensational performer in the whole world, Bollywood's divine light, The Pasha of Performance, The King of Romance, The Jackson of Action, currently ranked No. 1 in acting in the whole world, Yusuf Khan.

On the car journey back from the function, Karl and Kunal wondered aloud where the organizers could have got such misinformation from. As Karl put it, even Kunal's father was better informed about them. Yusuf Khan listened to this exchange, smiled broadly, and said, 'The difference between truth and untruth is just one letter.'

Karl: Actually, it's two letters.

Karl made sure he wasn't heard, as it slowly dawned on both of them that they were sitting right beside the source, the very crucible of misinformation— Yusuf Khan, the Hollywoodstani.

On another occasion, in Jodhpur, a fan managed to break the public barrier, rush to Kunal on the dais, and ask breathlessly, 'You are Mr Kunal?' Kunal replied in the affirmative and wished immediately that he hadn't. The fan's reaction to this news was to plant a kiss right on Kunal's lips. Kunal reacted exactly as a man would when a drunk male fan kisses him on the lips. He fainted. Karl and Yusuf couldn't stop laughing for months. The scars remain; even today if Kunal is asked for an autograph, his immediate reaction is to cover his lips first before reaching for a pen. Sadly, as Karl observed later, Kunal did this with female fans too.

As the two boys gained in popularity, an explosive new development took place, and this time it wasn't a Yusuf Khan script. The whole world had just been hit by a disastrous bug that was definitely going to alter people's public behaviour. Just as Neil Armstrong's nine-inch step in 1969 was a giant leap for mankind, this nine-inch instrument was a giant leap in communication technology. The mobile phone was worse than the plague of medieval times. Unlike when hit by the plague, mobile users not only continued to live, they often went on to get married, raise a family, and live happily ever after, all the while informing the entire world about their present state of affairs. Peace, quiet, and solitude were shattered. Silence and decorum in public places died grisly deaths. Restaurants, libraries, auditoriums, airports, sidewalks, funerals, and investiture ceremonies drowned in mobile phone activity.

Jehaan had a theory. He told the boys that mobile phones were part of a master plan by an alien race to take over the world. Kunal agreed, and said he even knew the alien race's name—Nokia. Jehaan ignored him and continued, 'Look at it this way, in a couple of years, everybody, rich or poor, big or small, old or young, will depend on mobile phones. Once that happens, the master alien race will start advising and instructing them through their phones.' Kunal replied, 'You know, you're right, it's already happening. It's called messaging.' This time Jehaan rose in a huff and stomped away, but not before warning the boys over his shoulder that their thoughts, feelings, and very existences would soon be monitored and controlled. Discussing Jehaan's opinions later, Karl and Kunal agreed that there was some truth to what he'd said. The mobile phone was becoming ubiquitous. Moreover, one's character and status were coming to be defined by the type of mobile phone one chose to use and display.

As the two boys tried to find a foothold in Bollywood, they got wind of the fact that India's greatest actor was actually shooting a scene at a set near theirs. The conversation that followed went something like this, and may rank among the loftiest verbal exchanges of the last century:

Kunal: Amitabh Bachchan's shooting on the next set.

Kunal: Oh my God!

Karl: Oh my God!

Kunal: Oh my God!

Karl: Oh my God!

Soon afterward, the two starstruck fans found themselves on a neighbouring film set. The scene was complex; Amitabh Bachchan had to emerge from a large pool of water (which was playing the part of Lake Michigan), engage in a lengthy dialogue completely out of breath, and then dive back into the water to continue his pursuit of a super-sized alligator with a voracious appetite that ate three human beings per minute. As far as Karl and Kunal could make out, the alligator was still to be cast. The director warned everyone to be silent as they recorded the sound.

On the magic word 'Action!', Amitabh dived into the water, and twenty seconds later he began to cut through the water's surface like a knife. Greg Louganis couldn't have done a better job. Consummate professional that he was, AB started on his breathless, lengthy dialogue, but just as he was swearing to save humanity from this dreaded creature, or to die trying, horror of horrors, a phone went off. The moment was shattered, and the director was livid.

Director: Who is the idiot? Who is the nutcase whose bloody phone is ringing? Who is the buffoon?

Calmly, Amitabh Bachchan opened a pocket flap in his wet shirt, pulled out his phone, and said—in his inimitable baritone and with impeccable timing— 'That buffoon is me.'

One day when Yusuf Khan presented the two boys with identical bright yellow phones the size of television sets, they found themselves in a dilemma. After all, they couldn't insult their benefactor, yet which self-respecting adult male who wasn't a leading fashion designer or ballroom dancer could actually walk around with a neon-yellow phone the size of Shaquille O'Neal?

Yusuf was one of those people who confused size with class. That was primarily because he had gifted a string of his girlfriends with breast implants. Yusuf owned the biggest phone in Mumbai. The running joke was that Yusuf's phone was so big that it was more of an immobile phone than a mobile one. The boys finally solved the problem by buying two smaller regular black phones for everyday use, saving the yellow ones only for their public appearances with Yusuf.

The Munshi Brothers' success meant that sequels had to be made. As they rose in Bollywood's pecking order, certain rules had to be followed.

Yusuf: Kunal, we need to give you a more bling image. You look too ordinary, and now you're a big star.

Kunal: I have a purple tie in my glove compartment...

Yusuf: No, no, we have to do something permanent to you to enhance your look.

Kunal: Dieting is out of the question, and I'm told liposuction has many side effects; on the other hand, I keep a purple tie in my glove compartment...

Yusuf: Arrey bhai, we'll need to find something more defining, more you, more Kunal. Earrings! Earrings! Earrings are the answer.

Kunal: You want me to wear earrings?

Karl: Yusuf, remember this is the guy who first became famous for being a watermelon, and now you want to add earrings to an oversized fruit? What is it today...er, friendship day?

Kunal: Yusuf, you wanna just take a look at the purple tie, it's...

Kunal didn't finish the sentence, partly because he realized he was running out of support, but more because Yusuf was throttling him while Karl repeatedly whacked his head with a newspaper.

A couple of days later, a gentleman who was 80 per cent tattoo and 20 per cent human visited the three of them on the set. With a pen-like instrument, he made a hole in Kunal's left earlobe. Kunal didn't react immediately. Then, a full two seconds later, he screamed like a woman having a difficult birth (this experience came in handy years later when he played the role of Mrs Iyer in *Mrs Iyer Aur Mai*). The crew outside the trailer ignored the cries, assuming that some whinning actress was being shown the ropes by Yusuf, the director, or by Kunal, or in all probability, by both.

After a few minutes, when the pregnant lady regained her composure, Karl casually remarked to Tattoo Man, 'Oops, we made a mistake, it's supposed to be in his right ear lobe.' Outside the trailer, some of the crew wondered why the starlet's initiation was taking longer than usual.

Okay, it's time to meet another important member of the film community. A person who guides and watches the actor, fills in all the roles from philosopher to friend and guide, and means more to the actor than his parents, directors, producers, and co-stars combined. I speak of the spot boy. So named for one of two reasons: (a) they can be spotted at any time, (b) the first spot boy ever invented back in the 1930s suffered from a very rare, permanent case of chickenpox, caused by his excessive exposure to the leading heroine of the time.

Yusuf Khan's spot boys (he had two, being a big star) were Mohan and Arun. Mohan had been with Yusuf from the very beginning, and being a bit of an auntie, saw himself as a mother-like influence on Yusuf's life. For his part, Yusuf had more respect for a common mosquito than he had for Mohan. He'd call out to Mohan using the universal Indian expression for disdain, the sound, 'ehh'. This stretched syllable used instead of a name was employed primarily to call people one couldn't care less about. Yusuf, for instance, would go, 'Ehh, I want lunch from China Eyes.' Mohan would respond with an expression of puzzled pain. He had had the same look when he was once made to sit through an entire Def Leppard concert holding Yusuf Khan's water bottles.

Yusuf: Which part of the order have you failed to understand, 'lunch', 'China', or 'Eyes'?

Mohan would now start to crumble like an old cookie. Arun on the other hand was young, dynamic, and a performer. He was employed when Yusuf was already a household name, when Yusuf had already gained notoriety as the 'King of Lifting' because of his habit of rehashing Hollywood hits and then denying the charge. Arun anticipated Yusuf's every move. For instance, Yusuf habitually wanted to use the bathroom right after lunch. Arun would swiftly ask everyone to leave the trailer, and clean the bathroom in anticipation of the inevitable. Mohan was kept on simply because of the loyalty factor. In truth, he just got in Yusuf and Arun's way.

Yusuf decided to gift Karl and Kunal a spot boy each.

Karl's spot (it's not as insensitive as it sounds) was named Satheesh. He got the job not because of a terrific track record and many years of experience, but on an even stronger recommendation. He was Arun's younger son. Kunal's spot Dharam was even more qualified in that sense, being Arun's elder son.

When Jim Morrison purred the lines, 'Like a dog without a bone or an actor all alone', he wasn't talking about Bollywood stars. Indian actors are never alone. Wherever they go, the spot boy is three steps behind. Even a man's shadow gives a man some breathing space, but spot boys are unrelenting. As always, Yusuf came to the rescue.

'Boys, let me tell you how to deal with spot boys. You have to pretend they don't exist. If you want or need something, ask for it aloud and know that you are the privileged one. God will hear your prayers and provide. How He chooses to provide is not your business. Just know that your wish will be granted. Of course, there are one or two exceptions. For example, once I was doing a long schedule in Malaysia, and feeling ill I asked God for a doctor, and the Provider sent me an adapter, an adapter switchboard, instead of a doctor. Consequently, I requested God not to provide anything through my servant Mohan and ever since I've relied heavily on Arun instead; as Arun unlike Mohan is far more old-fashioned and uses his ears for listening.'

As the boys began getting used to the perks and trappings of Bollywood, the Munshi Brothers were going great guns. After the success of the first two Munshi Brothers films, Yusuf decided to raise the ante, lift the bar, or, as the saying goes, push the envelope. Having lifted and incorporated every single frame from the Marx Brothers in his earlier efforts, Yusuf felt obliged to change, do something different. After all, he could hear the whispers and, worse still, with the advent of satellite TV, the actual Marx Brothers films were also available to the public. Having discovered a final, slender thread of integrity within

159

himself, Yusuf decided that for the third film in the Munshi Brothers series, he would curtail the lifting of material from the Marx Brothers. In fact, this time he was determined to lift only 20 per cent of the film's material from the Marx Brothers. The other 80 per cent would be split equally between scenes lifted from James Bond films and the Pink Panther series.

The plot thus roughly traced the tale of three brothers who are reunited as spies for the Indian government, and end up chasing a Russian gang of purse snatchers who turn out to be gorgeous supermodels with gorgeous accents, whose headquarters are in Paris. At the end of the film, the Russian supermodels, it turns out, are not Russian. In fact, they are not supermodels either. And neither are they females, but are in fact the camouflage wing of the FBI who specialize in the art of disguise and who are hot on the trail of a diamond smuggler, the richest man in the world. The latter was born in Surat but now lived in France where he could easily be identified by his Surati accent, especially when he said 'wee', which is French for 'yes', Belgian for 'no', and British for 'urine'.

Everyone loved the script, chiefly because if you ever told Yusuf that you didn't, he would narrate the entire thing to you, a process that took a minimum of three hours. This script had two ingredients that Karl and Kunal had not experienced so far. Fighting and France.

It's time I introduced another august personage into my narrative. He was about six feet tall thanks to his four-inch heels. His trousers were too tight to have been put on him using conventional means. They must have been stitched on him after he stood upright. He had on two vests with a large black bush shirt, which gave him a thickset and menacing look. In fact, at first glance, he really did look quite menacing. It was the feet that gave him away—silver, pointed, high-heeled shoes were supposed to have gone out of fashion along with Mithun and Liberacci years ago… Nobody knew his real name, but he was called either Masterji or Sylvester Sir. Masterji because he was the fight master, and Sylvester Sir only if you were absolutely piss drunk, high on amphetamines, and visually impaired, when you might agree that at certain angles and under certain conditions of light and shade, namely, when it was pitch dark, you might just mistake him partly for Sylvester Stallone. Now, since the lighting was pretty good, let's just call him Masterji. Masterji always had four cronies who dressed exactly like him, and attended to his every word. They even had names that sounded the same—Babloo, Daboo, Ladoo, and Gaddu.

For their first fight sequence, Karl and Kunal, their heads covered in cloth and their feet bound, were escaping from the dreaded 'E Street Gang'. The entire shot was to be photographed from trees above the actors. As the scene unfolded, all the actors and extras were on the ground and all the technicians were in the trees. The scene basically had a gagged and bound Karl and Kunal trying to escape from the clutches of Evil. Just as they were about to be recaptured, Yusuf would enter the frame and save the day.

Masterji: You boys don't worry; we will chase you

and start beating you. Because we are trained, you won't feel the punches. Watch this.

He then began to demonstrate how to pull a punch. Basically, you aimed a punch at a person and just before you made contact, you pulled your hand back, creating an optical illusion that you had punched when, in reality, you hadn't. This was okay in theory, except that Sylvesterji was no good at it. Babloo, Daboo, and Ladoo all went down with the punches, while Gaddu excused himself from the proceedings with an imaginary phone call.

As the shot commenced, the nervous boys ran like headless pigeons in the agreed direction. However, the onslaught from Masterji and the others never came. This was because Kunal's face cloth fell off during the first take, and some onlookers recognized him as the famous comedian Kunal. Not seeing any cameras or crew and sensing trouble, they rushed to Kunal's defence. Sylvester and friends got the hiding of their lives. Masterji lost two front teeth, suffered a minor concussion and a rib fracture, Babloo had bruises all over. Daboo was nearly hung with his own belt, a fake Dolce and Gabbana that Masterji had gifted him. Luckily, the belt broke before the hanging was completed. Ladoo was stripped to his underwear, and Gaddu seized this opportunity to run away and pursue what he really wanted to pursue—Kathakali and Bharatnatyam. By the time the misunderstanding may have been cleared, it was too late. Masterji's shirt, shoes, and reputation were in the gutter, and while you can replace a shirt and a reputation, four-inch high-heeled silver shoes with pointed fronts are utterly irreplaceable. The crowd, which was part of a passing Ganpati procession, was difficult to control. They only calmed down once Yusuf Khan made an appearance and promised he'd use all of them in his film. He was delighted that even with an entire fighting crew and extras wiped out in one cruel stroke, the schedule for *Munshi Brothers in Paris* would not be disrupted.

The matter didn't end there. The procession insisted that the rescued stars join them. Kunal was worried that the three-hour walk to the sea was two hours and fifty-seven minutes too long for him, while Karl had a sneaky feeling that once at the sea, seeing Kunal was twice the size of the idol, the procession might feel tempted to immerse him instead. Finally, after much begging and pleading and a promise that Yusuf Khan would chair all their society meetings every Friday for the next seven years, the crowd moved on and so did *Munshi Brothers in Paris,* but without its fight department.

All this paled in comparison to what awaited the boys in Paris, the city of love, or as it's called by Indian tourists, the city that refuses to respond to English. The taxi driver from the airport quickly gave them the lowdown on France. 'Most French people today look like me; ethnic white Frenchmen are almost extinct. Not more than three or four are left in Paris. Most of them are concentrated in a village near Dijon, although I'm told there are at least five families in France's southernmost state, Pondicherry.'

In spite of their star status, the boys were put up at a small hotel that was probably a cross between a motel and a hotel with the resultant offspring carrying more of the motel gene. The very name should have warned them. I mean El Dorado is hardly the sort of name you'd associate with a French hotel.

The rooms were approximately six inches shorter than the average shoebox. When Karl stepped into his, he found that he stepped out of the window almost immediately. This was because the main door and window were closer than Hugh Hefner is to his Playboy Bunnies. It consisted of a bed and…well, that was it, just a bed. Once on the bed, Karl spread his legs and did the impossible—he touched the main door with one foot, and the window with another. From end to end, any point in the room could be reached by his legs.

Worse was to follow. The bathroom was more bath than room. Above the pot (and here's when you know you are in a refugee camp, not just a Third World country), directly above the pot, hovered the smallest shower in the world. It was at best the size of an ear bud, and it was placed directly above the pot. This meant that you were probably expected to use the toilet and shower at the same time. Just as our ancestors Homo-not-so-Erectus, Homo-I-can't-be-bothered-to-do-this, and Homo-let's-use-the-river-for-everything used to do millions of years ago every Tuesday.

Kunal's problems were infinitely worse. The bed just wouldn't accommodate his girth. And then, Kunal, with his particular need to sit while bathing, left a characteristically Indian stamp on the hotel by exerting undue pressure on the pot lid and eventually going right through it. There's an old Sanskrit saying

164

that you can put an Indian anywhere in the Western world on a Western toilet and he'll destroy it completely in seconds. Kunal was no exception. Every time he collected his room key or mail from the reception desk, he was met by employees with hands covering their mouths, making gurgling and giggling sounds. He learnt much later this was French for laughter.

The Eiffel Tower song was the climax of the boys' Paris humiliation. In the first scene, the boys were placed on either side of the tower, and they had to continuously run in and hug parts of the tower. Kunal was delighted that his prediction about Karl's love for 100-year-old women was coming true. His joy was blotted out when he was told that he too had to follow suit. This was followed by more shots of obeisance—kneeling in front of the tower, kissing the tower, cleaning the tower, and performing an aarti on the tower.

The refrain for the Eiffel Tower song was in English and went like this:

Eiffel Tower, Eiffel Tower,
You are my cover, lover, flower,
Eiffel Tower, Eiffel Tower,
You are my shower, mower, power,
Eiffel Tower, Eiffel Tower,
I'm here you're there, I'm there you're here.

That particular summer, more tourists were scared away by the song's refrain than by the leptospirosis scare in 1962 or by Boy George in 1985.

In the history of the world, a few things such as extramarital affairs, male egos, and the acquisitive

165

instinct have always spelt trouble. But all of them are small change compared to the French accent. Medieval Europe was constantly going to war because of this accent. The Hundred Years War started when Andre Boheme, the French ambassador, had a meeting with his English counterpart, Pascal Huffings. All Boheme meant to say at the meeting was a simple 'Greeting to your King O Pascal.' However, with his French accent, it sounded more like 'Greetings to your King that rascal.' The result? War for a hundred years, with only Sundays and every second Saturday off.

Munshi Brothers in Paris also ran into language difficulties. As director of photography, Yusuf had hired the leading French cameraman Jeremy Challaeux. Jeremy was 8 feet 1 inch tall and hard of hearing in the left ear. He also had a peculiar affliction—he was almost blind. This is not the best of physical impairments for a cameraman. Since two of his faculties were almost totally defunct, Jeremy relied greatly on his sense of smell. It was said he smelt out a location and used his nose to create some of the greatest visuals in cinematic history. Take the case of the filming for *Le Butterfly e D'winge* (*The Butterfly Has Wings*) in which he shot the Leaning Tower of Pisa in a way that made it appear absolutely straight. For this film, he won seventeen awards, of which there were at least three he hadn't paid for. Yet his detractors maintained in hushed whispers that Jeremy had no idea where he had placed the camera, and that the erect Tower of Pisa was just a lucky shot.

The other problem was that Jeremy often received instructions in the wrong ear, which was much the same as talking to a stone, and had exactly the same result. Things reached a head when there was a fire on the set and someone yelled into Jeremy's wrong ear that he ought to flee. The shooting came to a standstill for three weeks, to allow Jeremy's burns to heal. But the only thing worse than Jeremy receiving instructions, was him giving them.

Jeremy: Yasoof, mooove heeem intoo zeee phountaain.

Yusuf: No way.

Jeremy: Just dooo eeat, mooove heeem intoo zeee phountaain.

Yusuf: I can't do that.

Jeremy: Eeef yoo don't mooove heeem, I weeel kameeet sooociiide.

Yusuf: I don't know what you're saying, but I can't move him into the fountain.

Jeremy: Ands why nought?

Yusuf: Because if I put him in the fountain, he'll drown. The fountain is twenty feet deep. If he goes in, we'll never see him again. He can't swim.

Jeremy: And zee negateeive point eeez?

Yusuf: I said no.

Jeremy: Yooo diagreee because your muzher and fozher are both cross-eyed camels, yooo are zeee grandson and speeting eemaage of a speeting llamaa. Yooo should close zeee pheelum and go join all zeee oder aneemals in Madagascar.

Yusuf (in Hindi): Thank you. Wish you the same.

Jeremy wasn't the only truth unravelled in Paris. Walking the city streets on off days, Karl and Kunal came to the following conclusions:

(a) Paris had far too many museums and art galleries—

far too many for a civilized person to tolerate.

(b) It soon became clear that the French Revolution took place because of these sundry art galleries and museums.

(c) The battle cry of revolution was in fact 'Liberty, Equality, Fraternity and, above all, Please Not Another Art Gallery'.

(d) Far too many paintings involved flowers. Heterosexual men can tolerate only so many flowers in a day.

(e) Heterosexual men prefer the nudes to flowers.

(f) The nudes suck!

(g) All the nudes have women with the proportions of dairy cows.

(h) Heterosexual men can tolerate only so many cows in a day.

(i) France's economy was built on one thing and one thing alone—souvenirs.

The last point really hit the boys hard. Everywhere they went, they were offered the same rubbish as souvenirs. A miniature Eiffel Tower! What idiot would, after seeing one of the largest wonders of the world, want to keep a three-inch replica of it in his pocket? Apparently there were plenty. The world wouldn't be running out of idiots any time soon. Then there was the postcard of the River Seine. Were those two inches of water really the River Seine, Karl wondered. It could quite easily have been the River Indus or Powai Lake or some water from a bucket in your grandma's house. And how do you benefit from four inches of the Louvre or Napoleon's bust? What kind of statue doesn't have arms and legs? But the

French still find it very aesthetic. And the tourists kept buying it.

Karl made a mental note that if he were ever in a position to influence India's economy, he would borrow the French idea of selling souvenirs.

Around the time they were shooting in Paris, a very important event occurred. In order to promote the film, Yusuf Khan organized a photo shoot with a leading Indian magazine, *L'unofficial*. Yusuf had chosen a rather original location for the shoot, and one he believed had hardly ever been captured on film before—the Champs Élysées. The shoot included Karl, Kunal, Yusuf, and the new female lead, Padmini. While the boys wore jeans and T-shirts, Yusuf wore, for reasons best known to himself, a New York Yankees baseball uniform.

Karl and Kunal found themselves involved in a new intellectual pursuit. Of late, the boys had developed an uncanny ability to wiggle their ears in time to a marching beat. The beat went 'left, left, left right left'. Only instead of their feet marching to the beat, they could get their ears to do so. It was a neat trick and won them many friends, particularly in France where friends were hard to come by because of the French accent. The boys were trying in vain to teach Yusuf this new trick, but frustrated that he couldn't move his ears by themselves, Yusuf had begun cheating by moving his jaw when the photographer appeared.

Karl was stunned. His ears stopped moving altogether. Meanwhile, Kunal's started moving at a feverish pace. Finally, he had to hold them down. Only Yusuf remained completely composed. Yusuf was a rare individual who could look both composed and idiotic at the same time, and carry it off with elegance and ease.

Yusuf: Meet Sophia, our photographer.

Sophia was a veritable vision. Karl was used to over-made-up pretty damsels at shoots, but this was the real thing. Besides being Indian, she had what Karl liked most—long black hair. Looking at her cascading hair, he felt a wave of desire and indecision. He couldn't decide whether he wanted to cover himself in that hair, swing from it like Tarzan, or simply braid it. Maybe she'd let him do all three. Kunal, on the other hand, had lost all control of his ears once again.

The first photograph (clearly suggested by Yusuf) had Yusuf bent over. That is, bent over in a leapfrog position, with Yusuf playing the frog and Kunal making an honest effort to leap. Kunal whose limb movements were restricted to not more than 2½ inches at a time, and who had a jumping range equal to that of the Ridley turtle's, in an epic effort, actually raised some of his girth off the ground and landed his ample groin on the back of the unsuspecting Yusuf's head. The meeting of Yusuf's head with Kunal's groin led to the shoot having to be called off on medical grounds. As Padmini ran off to console Yusuf by promising she'd do a bit of leapfrogging of her own for him in private, Karl was left alone with the beautiful Sophia.

Sophia: Does this happen often?

Karl: It's normally safer to allow a two-year-old to cross a highway on his own than to allow Kunal to do anything remotely athletic.

Sophia: Really? Anyway, I hated the damn shot. Yusuf really shouldn't be allowed to frame shots.

Karl: Yusuf shouldn't be...allowed, period.

At this they both laughed and somehow wound up at the local 'boulangerie', sipping coffee. It was then that Karl realized that one of the qualities on which he prided himself most suddenly threatened to humiliate him. Like his father before him, Karl believed in never carrying money. To quote Jehaan, 'Money is like a gun, if you carry it, sooner or later you'll have to use it; if you use it, you'll always end up regretting that you did.' While not quite as lyrical as Keats or Shelley, Jehaan could still be persuasive. Much to his chagrin, Karl realized that beautiful and charming as Sophia was, her appetite was considerable. Karl gaped, as Sophia wolfed down a lamb quiche the size of Beijing, a lemon pie, some poorer member of the lasagne family, three cups of coffee, and a mince pattice. As Karl watched this Olympic performance, he began to panic and as always, when he felt a sense of panic, Karl needed to bang his head against something hard. In desperation, he chose the coffee cup, which would have worked out fine if it didn't have any coffee in it. Momentarily stunned, and then violently scalded, Karl hopped and screamed and finally rushed out of the café.

Soon, he was sitting on the sidewalk with Sophia caressing his burnt forehead and limbs with ice wrapped in a handkerchief. In a soothing, maternal voice Sophia said something that eased Karl's pain immediately: 'Don't worry Karl, I've already cleared the bill.' For Karl, the moment was almost spiritual

171

in its intensity. But even as Karl's spirits soared, Kunal crept up behind them, now fully in control of his ears. 'Where did you guys go? Why are you icing him all over? Whatever, c'mon guys, let's go for coffee.' Karl cringed at the very mention of the word.

Karl: No, man, no, I think she's had enough, I mean we both have...

Kunal: C'mon man, I need to feed the animal (pointing to his stomach).

When Karl and Kunal had an awkward moment they would both rely on the word 'man' to prop up the conversation. Karl wouldn't budge though. As Karl and Sophia's relationship blossomed in the days ahead, there would be more instances when Kunal felt a little let down. Henceforth, ever so occasionally, the animal would have to feed itself.

Feeling that he hadn't made a good enough impression on Sophia, Karl was hellbent on setting the record straight. They went on a frenzy of dates, mostly without Kunal. As Karl tried to increase his brownie points, he found fate conspiring against him. Like the time that they went to the cemetery in Paris with, inter alia, Jim Morrison, Victor Hugo, Oscar Wilde, and four million termites. Karl could not help thinking how convenient it was that these famous names didn't have to pay rent. Sophia being a far more sophisticated and well-read mademoiselle was quick to disappear among the dead and buried. Her last words were, 'Meet me at the fifty-fourth tombstone.'

All this was fine until three things happened. First, it began to grow dark. The darkness had a menacing, ghoulish quality to it, and there were occasional silver-violet streaks of lightning and thunder that would have put a Bollywood movie to shame. Immediately, Karl felt a strange dampness, though he couldn't quite ascertain whether it was from the rain or himself. Second, the epitaphs and tomb markers around him were mostly in French; many were in ancient Gaelic, and some were in what seemed to be a hybrid of Malayalam and Cantonese. Finding number 54 was never going to be easy. Third, as he was searching for Sophia or number 54 or just a living face, a sharp sound made him spin around. It was a groan, or to be more exact a prolonged moan with a distinct trace of heartfelt anguish. Its softness made it especially terrifying. As he turned, there stood before him a large mackintosh. And then, the coat spoke. 'Come here.' Karl's blood froze and not a word escaped his lips in fear. The voice grew more menacing. 'Come here.' But Karl stood rooted to the spot, too frightened to approach or flee. The mackintosh advanced towards him, and he tried to think of something unusual to steel his nerves. 'If I die here, I suppose I will have saved my family the transport costs.' But this line of thought only accelerated his panic. And all the while the mackintosh inched closer. So this was it, this was how one's final moments felt, thought Karl. Goodbye cruel world. Adios amigo. Sayonara. There was so much left to be done, that he'd never got round to doing. But the mackintosh interrupted his thoughts. 'It's only me, tiger,' rebuked Sophia mildly as she peeked out of her raincoat. But the damage had been done. Karl's macho image had been annihilated, and he was reduced to a mumbling, bumbling fool.

In college, Karl's friend Iqbal had had a theory. He said that if the hair on your arms stood up at a girl's touch, it meant you really, really liked her. At the time, Karl and Kunal had not taken Iqbal seriously, possibly because he had last scored only 23 per cent in his science exam. Years later, sitting in a movie theatre, watching *Rome*, a film he had seen seventeen times already, Karl pondered Iqbal's statement. At one point, his arm grazed Sophia's wrist. Karl withdrew his arm immediately and checked the damage. Nothing, not a hair had stirred. Five minutes later, he tried the experiment again. A quick touch and back to base. But once again the results were nil. Four tries later, he decided to abandon his efforts. But he happened to cast a surreptitious glance in Sophia's direction, specifically at her arm, and lo and behold, the hair on Sophia's arm was standing. Karl was stunned. At first he wasn't sure what stunned him more, the fact that her hair appeared to be standing, or that Sophia actually had hair on her arms in the first place.

Confused, but also relieved and happy, he decided to focus on other matters for the moment, and silently shifted his attention to the popcorn. With his confidence in his own charm gradually returning, he couldn't help but wonder if there was a little hair on the popcorn that was standing too.

chapter 8

'Relationships are like underwear—the more you use them, the more comfortable they get.' So said Colsten Shakespeare, in case you want to do a background check. Sophia had followed Karl to India, and soon they started going off on romantic weekends to Goa, Kerala, Mahabaleshwar, etc. Karl's philosophy about weekends was simple: (a) the place must have air-conditioning, (b) it must have cable TV, and (c) it must have bubble bath facilities. Karl believed that if these three options were available, he could easily survive a weekend with Atilla and the Huns, let alone someone he was actually growing rather fond of.

Quite obviously, Karl and Sophia's relationship had progressed far beyond the harmless coffee shop stage. Nonetheless, to fund his girlfriend's excessive appetite for food, Karl had begun to carry money with him occasionally. As an actor, he had certainly grown in leaps and bounds. Well, that wasn't quite true. As an actor, he'd gone nowhere, but his career had certainly taken off very well. In eight years, he'd done 22 films, one of which was an 'art' film about an Indian boy who fell in love with a Hungarian girl settled in America. But his other 21 releases were all blockbusters, all part of the Munshi Brothers series, and all co-starred Yusuf and Kunal. To top it all, Karl and Kunal were regularly signed up for ads for products ranging from shoes to soft drinks and even soaps.

Advertising in India had entered a boom phase. Ads were being churned out faster than Cher's body parts. Film stars, sports stars, and relatives of ad executives were used to endorse products most frequently. Naturally, brands tried to match their image with that of the celebrity.

Enter a new two-in-one soap-cum-shampoo called Doubles. Doubles targeted the middle class south Indian woman who wouldn't have to buy both a shampoo and soap any more, once she settled for Doubles. India's leading ad filmmaker Prahlad Kakkar had a brainwave. Prahlad Kakkar was a man who wore many hats. By this I don't mean that he did many things but that he literally owned 77 hats and wore two or three simultaneously. Hats of course never really interfered with his brainwaves. This time he thought why not use famous couples to endorse the brand? He settled on two famous pairs—tennis doubles champions, Mahesh Bhupathi and Leander Paes, and Karl and Kunal.

Prahlad Kakkar asked Karl and Kunal over for a chat. Within seconds of entering his office, the boys were impressed, because almost all the women in the office had ample bosoms. This, and the fact that Prahlad always wore a black Stetson, somehow placed Prahlad at the very top of his profession.

Prahlad embellished his conversation with lots of expletives. Wait, that's not fair…make that, Prahlad

176

embellished his expletives with a little conversation. Taken aback by all the unnecessary profanity, Karl made an unusual request.

Karl: Prahlad Sir, can you please stop referring to us as assholes, please?

Prahlad took one look at both of them, and apologized immediately.

Prahlad: I'm so sorry. I really abuse too much, didn't mean to offend you guys…so no more assholes… okay, so you bastards, you *have* understood the concept, right?

The shoot was incredible. Mahesh and Leander played against Karl and Kunal in an absurd Grand Slam Final called the Indian Open. After the match, all four rushed to the showers where the victorious Mahesh and Leander found the shampoo and soap missing. To their chagrin, in a nearby shower, the only soap-cum-shampoo nestled lovingly in Kunal's hands. After a series of errors, the four men showered in the same cubicle, starring Doubles, the unique soap-cum-shampoo.

Critics hated the ad, but social commentators said that the ad did more for the gay rights movement than anything ever witnessed in India earlier. The ad helped soap sales soar. However, one unfortunate consequence was that after sharing a soap-cum-shampoo in full view of the public, Leander and Mahesh's relationship started falling apart. There are some things you just can't live down, try as you may. Of course, Karl and Kunal had no such problems as they had been bathing together since they were toddlers. They also gained a reputation for being the cheapest brand ambassadors, as they were the only Doubles representatives who actually collected their free quota of soaps from their sponsor every week.

At the end of the long shoot, Prahlad Kakkar made their day by saying, 'With such poor acting skills and even poorer screen presence, both you guys are destined for years of success in the film world.'

Kunal and Prahlad continued to grow closer as friends over the years when they realized that other than buxom women and ridiculously ill-fitting hats, they had a third passion in common. Food.

With the fortune made from films and ads, Karl bought himself a small bungalow, which, as a tribute to where the moolah came from, he called Munshistaan. In the last few years, he had won many awards such as the Golden Peacock Award for Best Actor in a Comedy Role for *Munshi Brothers Part 8*, also known as *Tequila Sunrise* (since no apt Hindi translation was available for 'tequila', it was referred to only by its serial number, eight).

Karl's friend Kunal had become huge, not just as a star but in terms of his sheer physical bulk. Kunal had had a string of relationships, but unlike Karl and Sophia, none endured. His success in the Munshi Brothers franchise led him to host a food show on a TV channel, which was a great success. He also won his share of awards, and two that stood out were the Porcelain Cow Award, for his inspired performance in *Munshi Brothers 13: Dog Day Afternoon*, and the best TV host award for his food show, *Khaana, Peena, Sona*. The former award had been invented to ensure that all major heroes won some award or the other every year. Hence, award categories included best comic performance, best tragic performance, best tragicomic performance, best villain, best villainous performance, best 'grey area' performance, and best performance in a bad role. Then, as they started running out of categories, they came up with best moment in film, most inspired performance, most awesome performance, etc...most stylish, most easy on the eye, most languid, most feline, most masculine, and so on. Kunal also built a bungalow right next to his friend's and called it Munshighar! Both bungalows soon became tourist attractions, and as Kunal grew both in width and stature, he realized he needed a bigger front gate.

This brings us to the third member of the trio Yusuf Khan. Yusuf Khan was a good twenty years older than the boys, and as the years rolled by, he was sad to find that he continued to remain twenty years older than them. He had sailed through the first seven Munshi Brothers releases at breakneck pace, only pausing for the out-of-court settlements with the Marx Brothers Foundation, for plagiarism. The payoff was huge and cost him the profits of his first five films. He also had to mention the source of his inspiration at the start of every subsequent film, like an errant schoolboy caught with his pants down. In his decree, before encouraging an out-of-court settlement, the judge said: 'Having reviewed the first five Munshi Brothers films against the Marx Brothers films, I find the two series to be exactly the same, and one is obviously a copy of the other. The only discernible difference is that the Marx Brothers are much better looking.'

Plagiarism wasn't the only thing bothering Yusuf. Age brought its own set of problems. Already almost bald on top and alarmed at the growing number of white hair, he even tried dyeing his hair green for a while. But the white reappeared, dividing the green into dark and light shades. Gossip columnists launched a discussion on the effects of cheap green dye. Insulting articles were published, including one that said, 'While one certainly needs to push for the world to go green, this really means the world minus Yusuf Khan.' Yusuf also began to grow a double chin—highly visible folds of flesh accompanied it, and that meant that Yusuf no longer wanted to be photographed from below. But his green hair made it virtually impossible for him to be photographed from above. The only solution was to have the camera film his right profile, and indeed in *Munshi Brothers 17*: *The Blue Lagoon*, his entire performance was captured in profile. Despite these problems, Yusuf Khan won the best actor award for fourteen consecutive years. Much like his two protégés, he bought a bungalow (his fifth) right beside theirs, and called it Munshibagh.

Sophia and Karl had now become quite the social pair, seen at parties, functions, and, for a price, at birthdays as well. Sophia was a trendsetter; if she wore red, the city wore red; if she wore burgundy, the whole city wore burgundy, except of course those who couldn't pronounce it. But the relationship wasn't welcomed equally by everybody. It all started at the cinema where Karl, Sophia, and Kunal had gone to watch a murder mystery. After a whole lot of twists and turns, gut-wrenching suspense, and pulsating thrills, the murderer was about to be announced by the film's protagonist. At that precise moment Kunal broke into a series of unstoppable coughing fits. The fits would start like machine-gun fire, and then after 4½ minutes, subside into short, sharp sounds such as those made by a squash ball when it slams into a wall. Kunal's performance drowned out the protagonist's. The whole theatre was incensed, demanding their money back, as they had missed out on the murderer's name. When the house lights came on and they recognized the stars, their stand softened, but not Sophia's.

Sophia: How embarrassing is that? Why don't you take something for that cough?

Kunal: It's not my fault. I just have a dry throat!

Sophia: Not your fault? The 50 cigarettes a day are not your fault?

Kunal: If I stop smoking, my cough gets worse.

Sophia: So what you're saying is smoking is medically beneficial; you use it to cure your cough.

At this point, Kunal started coughing again, almost on cue.

Rather hurt by Sophia's brusqueness, Kunal tried to occupy himself by turning to what he abhorred most—sports. Golf took far too long, and besides, the clubs were too heavy. Chess on the other hand meant too much concentration, and being in the same position for more than seven minutes was always a challenge for his back, except when he lay absolutely flat on his back, in which case he could remain in the same position for days on end. Rugby was too masculine, badminton and table tennis called for

181

too much deft movement, and bridge forbade the wearing of shorts. The only sport that remained accessible to him then was gargling, and here he was the undisputed champion, with the most unusual ability to belt out the national anthem while gargling at the same time. (In the sport of gargling, the central idea is to churn out popular musical hits with clear enunciation and pronunciation, and most importantly without once spilling the liquid from one's mouth. It is considered an extreme sport and shouldn't be tried out except under expert guidance.)

Given his limited interest in sports, and even more limited sporting ability, Kunal decided to do his bit to revive English theatre in the city. Karl suggested that perhaps this was best done by Kunal staying away from it. Kunal, however, believed that if he acted like a neo-age impresario, the crowd would flock to the theatre once again. He founded a theatre outfit called Flesh and Bones. As a rotund young boy, Kunal had often been described as all flesh and no bones. These remarks had scarred him deeply. Uniting 'flesh' and 'bones' harmoniously was his idea of... er, payback.

Kunal then announced Flesh and Bones' first theatrical venture, *Romeo and Juliet*. Karl suggested that Kunal play both characters to do justice to his girth. Kunal contented himself with playing just one, Romeo—possibly, the largest Romeo of all time.

It was around this time that Sophia called Karl to a coffee shop for the 'Talk'. For males, 'Talk' is one of the most frightening words in the English language. History abounds with examples of the Talk causing grievous injury to august individuals. Hannibal, for one, after receiving the Talk from Mrs Hannibal-to-be (name withheld on request), tried unsuccessfully to throw himself off the Alps. Peter the Great, after his Talk tried to commit suicide by translating Chekhov into English. Horatio Nelson took ballet classes out of sheer humiliation. Only Henry VIII had the clarity of thought, vision, and sense of justice to chop off his ladies' heads after the Talk.

What was it that he liked about Sophia, Karl kept asking himself. Eventually, he had decided to ask his father, and found Jehaan more than forthcoming. 'Son, I've survived many hundreds of marital battles with your mother, and now I'm going to tell you how. First you must master the three magic words.'

Karl: I love you?

Jehaan: No, you idiot. 'Yes', 'no', and 'sorry'. These three words have saved more marriages than separate TVs. When you answer your wife's questions, just reshuffle these words until you get a favourable response. For example, if your mom asks me, do you think Aarti is prettier than me? I always say, 'No.' She then says, 'Are you sure?' And I reply, 'Yes.' She then says, 'But I caught you looking at her?' And I end with, 'Sorry'. There. Marriage saved. The other thing is, if you want to take the relationship further, you need to go out a lot.

Karl: But you and Mom never go out.

Jehaan: Of course we do. I go out on Tuesday and Mom on Thursday.

The conversation ended with Jehaan giving his protégé one last piece of advice. 'There is only one difference between man and woman, and this is it. If you ask a man, "How was your day?", he'll grunt or answer in a monosyllable. If you ask the lady, you'll get a fifteen-minute-long monologue, beginning with, "We got up ten minutes late and my son nearly missed the school bus, and so I was late to the gym, so I had to wait in line for the treadmill and you won't believe Seema was on it and everything she was wearing was in black, even then it didn't hide her paunch, and can you believe she was in shorts even though she hadn't waxed her legs. I mean if one is really her friend, one should tell her but..."'

Luckily by then Karl had, like the great Elvis Presley, left the building. He still wasn't sure what he liked about Sophia, but for the first time he realized, sometimes the details don't matter.

Now, let's listen closely to a sample of the 'Talk', the thought of which unnerved Karl so.

Sophia: Karl, we need to talk, and I mean talk.

Karl: (Teeth chattering)

Sophia: My parents are asking, you know.

Karl: Do you have some money?

Sophia: Yes. Why?

Karl: I'll need some coffee first.

Sophia: Fine. Two coffees please. Karl, we've been going around for ages, it's time for the next step, I think.

Karl: Er...I'm not feeling too well.

Sophia: I'm talking marriage, Karl. I don't want to be one of those women who have children in their fifties.

Karl: I'm not quite ready...maybe in ten or twenty years...

184

Sophia: Don't talk rubbish. It's NOW or NEVER, Karl.

The last two words were spat venomously.

Karl: Can't we think about this for a little while?

Sophia: Define 'a little while'.

Karl: I don't know, a year, six months, a week at least...

Sophia: No, we are getting married as soon as possible.

Karl: Sophia, can we cancel the coffee, I think I need something stronger.

Sophia: Oh! I'm so happy, darling, let's go tell everybody the wonderful news. I still can't believe you proposed to me.

Karl (body parts exchanging positions): I'm really not feeling well, I think I need to lie down.

And so, just like his father before him, Karl responded to the news of his marriage like a man—by lying down in a coffee shop and pretending he had died. The next day, the papers were filled with stories of the star's impending marriage. Several papers also had cartoons of Kunal dressed as a watermelon crying at the news.

Big events tend to behave like hurricanes. They sweep all before them. Karl tried to slow down the process, but no matter how many times he lay down—at the caterer's, at the dress designer's, at the florist's, or at the proposed venue, Sophia simply ignored him and carried on like a U-boat on the rampage.

Now what happened to Karl next happens to most straight men when faced with the possible trauma of marriage. He started having minor blackouts. He seemed to see things through a haze, and he couldn't always comprehend what was happening around him. Of course, these are normal reactions to marriage, and were hardly any cause for concern. His family observed that every time his marriage was mentioned, he would sneeze, throw back his head and mimic a drowning man trying to breathe. Being sensitive to his plight, his good friend Kunal began demonstrating this act to the general public, in the process making a tidy sum on the side. Yusuf Khan was genuinely delighted at the news of Karl's upcoming marriage, and in true filmi style, he shed copious tears of joy.

On a cool January evening, the wedding reception was held in a large open park. Hundreds of people attended the wedding and, as is usually the case at Indian weddings, 90 per cent of them didn't know either the bride or groom. One of the highlights of the evening was a drunk Kunal's soulful rendition of Jehaan's favourite Neapolitan song, 'A'Vuchella', into a microphone. This was followed by Yusuf Khan's recitation of a poem that he had written for the occasion.

Sophia and Karl are like the sky and the rain
They spend all the time avoiding pain,
Now they'll see each other again and again,
It should be enough to drive a normal couple insane...

Nobody waited long enough to hear the second verse. Karl himself was heard muttering under his breath that he'd prefer the damn marriage to another line of the poem. As is always the case at Indian weddings, the spread was sumptuous, grand and infinite. Sophia's parents cried, Karl's parents danced, and Kunal's father coughed the night away. The next morning, Karl woke up with his teeth chattering, heart pounding, and sweat pouring. With great trepidation, he opened his eyes and glanced at his right hand. The ring on his fourth finger confirmed that yesterday's events had not been some ghastly nightmare. He really was married.

Karl's first act as a married man was no different from that of most married men before him. He reached for a Crocin. Self-actualization, often confused with masturbation, comes to just a handful of lucky souls. Dr Barry White defines it as the process by which a person, having attained all material goals can achieve an intangible, spiritual growth. His contemporary Dr Sashikant Wellingkar defines it as finding one's body parts in a dark room without cheating by using a torch. Be that as it may, let us examine Karl as he enters his thirties.

His career as an actor had brought Karl fame, fortune, and the occasional plastic surgery. Wealth and a certain social standing were now his, and that explained why he seemed to be on the lookout for something more.

His relationship with Sophia was excellent. They decided at the very outset not to have children. This was not a selfish choice, but a very mature one. Instead of children they had teddy bears, and after a while they got themselves two dogs. Munshi was a black and tan German Shepherd, and Ballsy was a jolly, round British Bulldog, with more than a passing resemblance to Kunal. The life of an actor, despite claims to the contrary, is a pretty stable one. Events such as changes in government, recession, calamities, assassinations, or second marriages rarely have any effect on them. Karl had reached a stage where he had actually started reading the newspapers again, and not just the matrimonial columns which he usually read to entertain himself with some novel Indian names and preferences.

But the moment of self-actualization is preceded by a sign or a revelation from above. Different people experience it in different ways, and the sign could range from being an accident to a terminal illness. For Karl, it was haemorrhoids. He began to suffer from piles. Physically, it was a painful phase, but it also left him enough time to think seriously about the nature of his existence and the quality of his life thus far. He was appalled at the shallowness of some of the things he had pursued so single-mindedly. Karl was convinced, however, that it wasn't too late to redeem himself. He knew he had to do something different, something meaningful. But what was it that he ought to do?

chapter 9

As he banged his head on the car's steering wheel, Karl felt a sense of peace begin to flow over him, and a while later his spirits lifted considerably. Something else Karl often did to soothe his nerves was to dig his nose. This was an art he had perfected, and after a little warm-up he could quite easily put up to three fingers into one nostril. Today, however, was not a good day for the Great Indian Nose Trick, as Mrs Parekh had been watching him from her car for well over two hours. You see, Karl and Mrs Parekh and the Sharmas, the Shahs, the Soonawallas, and in fact everybody who lived in south Mumbai between Worli and Walkeshwar had been stuck in the same spot for two hours and seventeen minutes.

The government or rather the municipality or somebody had decided to repair a pipe on Peddar Road. Nobody had ever seen the pipe. Peddar Road residents, both dead and living, were interviewed. None had ever encountered any such pipe, although one Mrs Subramanian from Kemps Corner had seen a rather long snake winding its way down a lane near her house.

Karl cursed the pipe. Thanks to it, all traffic going to and from Peddar Road had been diverted through

Malabar Hill. The result? People in the area were fast closing in on the world record for staying put in one spot for three hours and forty-seven minutes, currently held by the citizens of a suburb of Hanover City in Germany. Karl was about to use the steering wheel to soothe himself once again when he noticed Mrs Parekh falling apart.

Now everybody knew that Mrs Parekh was part housewife, part plastic. As her car's air-conditioning faltered, Mrs Parekh began to come undone. Karl watched in amazement as layers of Mrs Parekh started peeling away. As pieces of what appeared to be terracotta and acrylic began to fall off her face, Karl decided it was safe to enter his nose. Brazenly, he dug into his nasal cavity, while parts of Mrs Parekh looked on helplessly. Since both their secrets were out, the two exchanged a look of mutual respect.

And then, something inside Karl snapped. He learnt later it was his seat belt, as he had leaned too far forward while digging. As he saw more and more of his neighbour disappear, Karl decided something had to be done. The city was a mess, the roads, the politics, the corruption, Mrs Parekh...they all needed to be put right. Someone had to do something. As Karl used his free hand to adjust the air-conditioning, he decided his time had come. After all, he didn't want to land up like most of Mrs Parekh, on the floor of the car, unsung, unloved, and utterly useless. With the elections two months away, now was the time for change, for a new direction, for new leaders, a leader with Napoleonic traits. A brilliant general, a strategist, academician, man manager, visionary, and a veritable bubble of charisma—a man with a little of Chandragupta Maurya, of Kautilya, of Churchill, and some of Mikhail Gorbachev. Yup, actually lots of Mikhail Gorbachev. What the country needed was a man who was well-read, astute, instinctive, methodical, and who could embrace both the past and the future, the East and the West. And that man was Karl Marshall. He spoke the last two words aloud like an American pizza commercial voiceover. He looked around to see if any occupants of the neighbouring cars sensed this great opportunity for Malabar Hill, for south Mumbai, for Maharashtra, for India…er, nay, for the world. Karl Marshall simply knew he had to enter politics, and the first thing Karl Marshall had to do was stop referring to himself in the third person. That would definitely distance him (er…Karl Marshall) from the common man, not to mention confusing the present writer. Yup, Karl Marshall had decided to join the party or, more appropriately, Karl Marshall had decided to plunge into the world of party politics, contest the upcoming election, and then rescue his city and ultimately the world.

Popularity comes at a price. All of a sudden, you are expected to multi-task. Besides being a star, you have to heal the nation, feed the poor, and mingle with ruling dynasties. Karl could cope with the first two, but he found the third tiresome on two counts. First, the dignitaries were never on time, and second, the dignitaries were never ever female.

Karl, however, felt honoured that he and Kunal had been invited to meet Bill Gates—no other actor including Yusuf Khan had made the cut.

It was a strictly black-tie affair, and when Bill Gates entered the room, all 30 guests lined up as if for a school uniform inspection. Gates went down the line shaking hands with all till he reached Karl and Kunal right at the end of the queue.

Master of Ceremonies: Mr Gates, these are two of our most famous actors, Mr Karl and Mr Kunal.

Bill Gates: How do you do?

Karl: Fine. Thank you.

Kunal: Sir, I'm a huge fan of yours. I've followed your meteoric rise, your acquisitions, occasional hiccups. I've read everything I could about you...I think you are absolutely fantastic.

Bill Gates: ...Er...

Kunal: Yes, is there something you'd like to say?

Bill Gates: Er... yes... could you kindly take your hand off my back?

Was that Kunal's most glorious moment? Not if you asked Karl. That came six months later when they were part of a band of A-listers who got to meet with President Bill Clinton at the Oberoi Hotel in New Delhi.

President Clinton was his usual charismatic self, back-slapping one and all, though clearly and quite justifiably favouring the ladies. Of course, most couldn't follow his southern accent and communicated with bouts of nervous laughter.

Clinton: Looks like India and China are sitting on an HIV time bomb.

Socialite A: (Not comprehending the accent, nervous laughter)

Clinton: I love the chicken tikka masala, how the hell d'you make it, puhleeze fill me in.

Socialite B: (Not comprehending the accent, more nervous laughter)

While the above nervous laughter therapy session proceeded, Kunal sauntered off to attend to one of life's greatest pleasures, The Pee.

Kunal closed his eyes as many of us do during the act. He was roused from his bliss by approaching footsteps. And then, he found Bill Clinton standing at the urinal right beside his. Behind them stood a formidable cluster of Clinton's bodyguards. There were ten of them, and they seemed to be of an average height of 7 feet 5 inches. All peered threateningly at Kunal, as he seemed to be the only potential threat to the President.

Kunal buckled under the menacing gaze of ten pairs of eyes. But worse was to follow. The 6 foot 2 statesman turned to Kunal and asked genially, 'How's it going, [pause] little guy?' Kunal nearly fainted in embarrassment. 'Little guy'! The world's most powerful man had just seen the world's least powerful tool. What if he told the world about it? What if he told the senate? What if he had a joint parliamentary committee from both countries...?Kunal zipped up and ran out of the toilet. The whole incident may well have been swept under the carpet, if only he hadn't told Karl about it. Unfortunately, Kunal did just that.

After the Clinton caper, Karl and Kunal hastily exited the hotel, and Kunal nearly gave his car coupon away to a swarthy, strangely attired individual, who he assumed was in charge of valet parking.

'Are you nuts? That's the crazy politician Nilesh Kane,' whispered Karl. Kunal withdrew the ten-rupee note in the nick of time.

'You met thee Cleenton?' asked Nilesh Kane.

'What is a cleenton?' said Kunal naïvely.

'Good answer, baba. Driver, gaadi lao.'

Karl and Kunal watched in amazement as a man who actually seemed uglier and more gaudily dressed than Nilesh Kane rushed to do his master's bidding. Kunal whispered to Karl, 'What's a nilesh kane?'

Karl: No idea. Let's check *Animal Planet*.

He was to check *Animal Planet* sooner than he imagined.

Karl usually found it difficult to distinguish between one politician and another. This was because of a peculiarity common to Indian politicians. They all wear the same clothes—white kurtas and pyjamas, the only slight variation being that the dhoti sometimes substitutes for the pyjama. Their affinity for pyjamas stems from the fact that Indian politicians do most of their work when India is sleeping, or as Kunal succinctly put it, when India is not looking. Elaborating on the problem of identification, Kunal once famously asked the press: 'I mean, can you tell one milk bottle from another?' Historically, it was the first instance of a public figure referring to politicians as milk bottles. The remark caused quite a stir, and the political community protested. The eminent MP, Nilesh Kane, called for a hunger strike, which he led for the better part of three hours, before leaving to attend the inauguration of the city's first Thai cuisine restaurant, Nine Spice.

The matter was resolved when Karl, Kunal, and Yusuf invited a cross-section of the political community for the launch of *Munshi Brothers 11: The Unbreakable*, though Yusuf Khan was known to have said off the record that after the 'milk bottle' controversy, the case for breastfeeding would get a much-needed fillip.

Karl Marshall the statesman now decided the time had come to give concrete shape to his grand plan of bettering the lot of mankind in general. Timing, they say, is everything. At this crucial juncture in Karl's life, he got a phone call from three-time sitting MP, Nilesh Kane.

Before we attend to that call, let's check up on Nilesh Kane. Unfortunately, the Nilesh Kane species doesn't get a mention in the *Encyclopaedia Britannica*. But *The Indian Politicians Almanac*, now in its seventeenth edition, does do him justice.

Nilesh Kane was a career politician. His father was a politician, his grandfather was a politician, and his great-grandfather had started the tradition, though at first his great-grandfather worked as a stable boy. Being allergic to horses, he once fell very ill. It was then that he was given a job as a gardener at the minor politician MN Joshi's house. Since Joshi lived in a one-bedroom flat, there wasn't any garden. So the gardener acted as a 'fetch and carry' man. Joshi grew very fond of his gardener who was the only person who stuck by him through all three of his major afflictions—Parkinson's, liver cirrhosis, and the carpal tunnel syndrome (CTS occurs when the median nerve of the hand loses its function, and is normally associated with people like chief guests and doormen who shake hands too often and too excessively). MN Joshi survived all his ailments. Ironically, Kane Super-senior was killed—while waiting for his master's medical report—when a ceiling fan in the dispensary unhinged itself and chose him for a target. Filled with guilt and remorse, Joshi adopted Kane's son, who happened to be Nilesh Kane's grandfather. Joshi pushed his man into politics, and the Kane family never looked back. Since Joshi was a Congressman, the Kanes quite naturally adhered to the same party. When Nilesh Kane's father died, he severed ties with the Congress and joined the other large political party, the BJP. Rumour had it that he switched allegiances for a price of 25 lakh. Nilesh himself told close confidants that he did it because he felt the Congress Party had lost its sense of direction, its vision, and was constantly clipping his wings. But when Nilesh contacted Karl, he sounded as if he were fed up with the BJP as well.

Nilesh Kane stood at five feet three inches, if he stood on his toes, which in fact was how he always stood. He had a muscular build and if you didn't know him, the animal you'd think he most resembled was a panda. Of course, once you got to know him, you were more likely to use words like rat, viper, or even vulture. Nilesh was proudest of two things about his appearance: (a) he had a handlebar moustache dyed as black as the night and (b) he still wore his grandfather's Kashmiri topi, which almost exactly resembled the behind of a sheep. His most common mannerism while talking was to pull the two ends of his moustache until they met over his nose, where he'd make them play a cat-and-mouse game, like an electrician trying to get two opposing electric cables to fuse together. He considered his hat lucky, and legend had it that he never removed it. Not in the shower, not during intercourse, not even at the hairdresser's. Nilesh Kane also had a perennial cold, which meant he constantly swallowed his own phlegm with a revoltingly slurpy sound while talking. Nilesh Kane himself came on the line:

Nilesh: Karl there? Nilesh here.

Karl: Nilesh there? Karl here.

Nilesh: Congratulations on your latest Munshi Brothers picture number 21, *Dog in thee Manger*. (Nilesh always pronounced the English word 'the' as 'thee'; research has shown 19 per cent of all Indians do the same.)

Karl: It's number 22 actually, but tell me, how can I help you?

Nilesh: Karl, Karl, Karl, thee world is in bad shape, thee country is crumbling, thee people are all calling for one thing...

Karl: Change?

Nilesh: No, food. After so many decades of freedom, we still don't have food for everyone. No food. No electric (the term 'electric' is also used by the same 19 per cent), no water. Do you know 79 per cent of thee Indians don't have direct access to water?

Karl: That's a lot of thirsty people.

Nilesh: Oh forget thirsty, what about bath? This 79 per cent of thee Indians can't take bath (again, 'take bath', a phrase uniquely used by the same 19 per cent). You know why thee foreigners are always saying, 'Dirty Indians, you dirty Indians'? It is because we are actually not taking baths. (The same 19 per cent would also typically say 'Why we are not taking baths?')

Karl: Why?

Nilesh: Because we don't have thee water. I am fed up, Karl. (To emphasize the point, he repeated 'fed up' seven times in quick succession.) The two major parties are not performing, so I've decided to clean up thee system.

Karl: Okay.

Nilesh: I want to start a new, clean party, a new political power, and I want your support.

Karl froze. This was the moment he had waited for his whole life. He felt destiny brush against him, though it could simply have been a cool draft from the air-conditioner.

Karl: That's very interesting, Nilesh, but I have no experience in politics.

Nilesh: Does a virgin have experience before marriage? Does this make them less suitable for marriage? Both my wives were virgins before marriage, you must know that?

Karl felt this was both too personal and a trick question. He decided to answer with a diplomatic cough that would have made Kunal's father proud.

Nilesh: Let us not talk about thee matter on the phone. Please drop by to my office any time this week, and I will outline my plan to you. But I want you, Karl. The party needs you. The country needs you, please think about the situation.

As Karl hung up, he had already made up his mind.

This was a sign from the Gods. Being a popular and successful actor was all very well, but leadership was where his heart lay. He couldn't ignore the signs; much as the very sight of Nilesh Kane repulsed him, he could sense that Karl Marshall and Nilesh Kane would slowly but surely set the country right. But first things first. What should he wear to the meeting at Kane's office?

For a man without a party and a dubious political future, Nilesh Kane had a huge office. His office in fact was an entire three-storey building. Karl felt at home immediately. It was just like a film set. There were hundreds of people, many of whom had no business being there in the first place. Nilesh Kane sat on a gold chair that couldn't have been any uglier. Next to him were his three greatest acquisitions—a large jade statue of Shiva the Destroyer, a picture of his two sons (both of whom looked exactly like him but four and nine kilos heavier respectively), and his government-sponsored bodyguard. A bodyguard was the latest status symbol among the rich and powerful. Many of those who weren't given government-sponsored bodyguards would hire private ones. Celebrities who were slightly lower in the pantheon of the wealthy, hired actors to pose as bodyguards. Nilesh's bodyguard genuinely looked the part, with an AK-47 wrapped around his grey safari suit. It was a law for all bodyguards to wear grey—this became pretty obvious to Karl immediately.

Nilesh Kane sprang out of the chair to greet Karl with the same kind of agility one would normally associate with a paralysed panda. After the customary hug, Kane called for garlands, sweets, and the traditional coconut. Without consulting Karl, he had already decided that Karl would be the newest and brightest addition to his new, yet unnamed political party.

Nilesh: What should we call thee party?

Karl: How about Kane Party?

Karl had meant this as a joke, accompanying the suggestion with a sly grin.

Nilesh: Brilliant idea. Brilliant.

Karl began to perspire.

Karl: Perhaps not. People will think it's undemocratic to have a single person's name as the entire party.

Nilesh was heartbroken and sighed aloud. His other supporters tried to make him see reason. One said it sounded like a corporation, another said it would be mistaken for one of those slippery private banks. By then, Kane had already had a vision of the President of India announcing the Kane Party of India as the single largest party in Parliament, and then requesting Nilesh Kane, its leader, to take on the Prime Ministership and form his cabinet. Nilesh had drawn up a list of people who had helped him, and who he felt should form his cabinet. Like a teacher from his prep school, Mr Shankardas. And his mechanic Fredrick who'd been repairing his cars for twenty years but never charged him, or that old movie usher Gangaram who used to let him into the Royal Theatre through the side door, gratis, so that he could watch English movies. It was only when his finger accidentally dipped into his hot cup of tea that Nilesh Kane was roused from his stupor and refocused on the meeting. It soon became abundantly clear that the agenda for the day was (a) to name the new party, (b) to convince Karl to contest elections, and (c) to get a good massage and back rub. One look at the masseuse convinced Karl he'd be concentrating only on the first two.

Nilesh came up with a brilliant idea for choosing the party's name. He asked all his supporters to write down their suggestion on a piece of paper. He then proposed to put all these names in a secret ballot. Nilesh would read out all the suggested names and ask for a show of hands. Thus, no one would know who contributed which name and, once the name was selected by the electoral process or universal adult suffrage, Nilesh would take the credit for the chosen name by saying that it had been his very own suggestion.

So the process began. Nilesh dug into a gold bowl with all the names and, after shuffling them, he lifted a piece of paper and read out the name 'Satya Party', and then 'Parivartan'. Then came a host of similar sounding options, most of which received very little support. And then it happened. Even as he said 'Pyjama Party', Nilesh Kane knew that this was the one for him. At its first mention, everybody in the room began to chuckle. When an irritated Nilesh mentioned that this might be 'his' suggestion, all hands in the room shot up. Karl Marshall was the first to raise his hand, and that was fitting indeed, because the Pyjama Party had been his idea.

Now let's pause a little to gather our thoughts and ready ourselves for a brief lesson in philosophy.

The Pyjama Party's manifesto and vision were drawn up in the next few days. Most of the ideas came from Karl Marshall. Nilesh Kane was happy to let Karl bask in the limelight, contenting himself with an occasional 'That was my idea'. Karl, for his part, wasn't even mildly affected; he was far too focused on becoming the next Mikhail Gorbachev. While bathing, he even kept searching for hidden marks and spots on his body that may have been hidden all these past years. Mysterious marks and spots that might indicate his predestined greatness as the leader of the free world. But other than three pimples and one blackhead there really wasn't much to write home about. To return to the philosophy lesson, Karl Marshall and Team Pyjama spent the next few weeks ironing out their ideals and agenda. Karl and Nilesh divided the workload. Karl set about hiring new young Wharton-returned youths to help give the party a more hep and modern image, while Nilesh Kane took on the onerous tasks of daily facials, fish reflexology, and moustache trimming in preparation for the day of triumph. Of course, Kane was especially upset that they wouldn't let him consume the fish after each of his fish reflexology sessions.

The Pyjama itself was to symbolize a pure and simple cover that would protect the nation, especially its vital organs, and the election symbol, the Nada (the pyjama's drawstring) would symbolize the binding and holding together of the whole country, just as the Nada held the Pyjama in place. Here they ran into a little engine trouble as Nilesh Kane wanted to model the Pyjama in some pre-publicity photographs. This was a dangerous act, as his stomach, which almost sagged to his knees, would cover the whole of the

Nada, and defeat the purpose of promoting it. Nilesh Kane argued that if the Nada could hold his stomach in place, it would control the largest problems of the country just as effectively. Almost on cue, Nilesh sneezed violently, and unable to bear its intolerable burden any longer, Nilesh Kane's pyjama nada snapped. As Nilesh's tummy tumbled downward flaccidly before his minions, he tried to keep a straight face like a scientist hard at work trying out different combinations and permutations, completely oblivious to the occasional failure. Nilesh's moment of shame had the immediate effect of clearing the room. All his underlings, needing desperately to release the storm of laughter that had built up, rushed quickly to non-Nilesh Kane zones. Fortunately, Karl Marshall had changed into a man who could meet all challenges head on. He dipped into his vast reserves of theatrical talent and evolved a hybrid of a laugh and a cough. It began as a laugh but soon turned into a cough, and then quickly reached a point where one couldn't tell which of the two it was. Finally, the cough began to sound so convincing that Nilesh Kane forgot his own pyjama problems and rushed to Karl's aid, patting his back with one hand while the other struggled to hold on to his stringless pyjama.

A publicity campaign followed. Kunal and Yusuf Khan were roped in. A tie-up between *Munshi Brothers 23: International Velvet* and the Pyjama Party greatly profited both parties. Further, a marketing firm and advertising agency were hired. The agency, O+N, was among the most successful in the country. They recommended a five-point publicity drive:

1. All employees, supporters, and fans of the party must wear pyjamas at all times.
2. The pyjama would be coloured purple, because (a) purple is a loud, attention-grabbing colour and (b) O+N had lots of purple linen left over from their last ad campaign for a major textile giant.
3. The nada would be thick and white to signify purity.
4. The nada would be worn outside the pyjama like a belt. This would also help Nilesh Kane who would wear a pre-stitched pyjama and have just the nada on display over it. It would never be threatened by the enviable Kane stomach.
5. The topi would be a Western-style baseball cap, visually incorporating the national bird, the national animal, and the national sport. This would be done by displaying a tiger riding on a peacock while engaged in a frenetic bout of field hockey, presumably with another tiger on another peacock, which would remain unseen.

O+N felt this Western touch would hint at India's potential as a new, modern, and competitive global power, while the national animal and bird (of which there are respectively three and two left in the wild), combined with the long-forgotten national sport, would create the necessary 'desi' pride.

The following were some of the various reactions to the new Pyjama Party.

The leader of the opposition, 87-year-old Hrishikesh Singa: Ha, ha, ha, ha, hewoooo, I need to hold on to something. (At this point, Mr Singa convulsed and doubled up with laughter, fell down a flight of stairs, and had to be hospitalized for three months.)

The leader of the ruling party, JJ Jagmohan: Only in a true democracy can a mentally disturbed man be allowed to form a political party without any fear. This is proof, if any is needed, of the performance of my party in upholding democratic and egalitarian traditions.

The leader of the left, Mr George Mathew: If you meet a member of the Pyjama Party, follow this step-by-step process: (a) shake his hand, (b) shake his nada, (c) ask him to look over his shoulder, (d) quickly remove his nada, (e) now wrap the loose nada around his throat, (f) pull the nada tightly, and (g) release the nada only when the subject turns blue or seven days have passed, whichever comes later.

Other people around Karl Marshall also had a little to say.

Karl's mom, Maria: My God, Karl, please don't fraternize with them. Whatever happens, don't bring them here. I don't want any of those tobacco-chewing, kurta-pyjama types with cheap waistcoats loitering around my house. What if they flick something? They'll definitely flick something. Look at their dress, that's the way people who flick something dress.

Karl's dad, Jehaan: I had a friend in school, Sameer. Sameer's dad was an MP. So he used to come to school with a siren on his Ambassador car. Son, if you become an MP, make sure you apply for two sirens. I always wanted to have my own siren, and I don't mean your mother... Also, son, you'll get your own rail and air pass, which allows you to travel free, so make sure they only put your surname 'Marshall' on it...then later on any family member can use it. I can't wait to drive up to Sameer's house with my own siren and free rail pass.

Kunal: 'Make sure you tackle the real issues, don't get fooled by that poverty nonsense. No one in India is really poor. See, in our country there are just two types of people, those who are rich and pretend to be less rich—they are the ones who don't disclose their income, keep a low profile, and pretend to have financial problems; and there are those who are rich and pretend to be richer—these are those high-profile people keen to be seen everywhere, who overestimate both their worth and their wealth. So forget about poverty. The last time I checked, there wasn't any poverty. In any case, who cares about us? Who is singing our song? I'm talking about our basic necessities. I mean, look at the price of cigarettes. Cigarettes aren't a luxury, they are a necessity. Who is going to keep cigarette prices down? What about parking? I own five cars now, and I can drive all five of them, but I can't find a place to park even one of them in south Mumbai. Karl, don't get blinded by non-existent issues like communalism, casteism, and poverty; cigarette prices and parking problems are the real issues. Focus on cigarette prices and parking problems and you'll gain plenty of public support and... (at this point, Kunal had one of his violent coughing fits, and broke into incoherent gurgles and gasps).

Yusuf Khan: I don't know whether to laugh or cry. Pyjama Party? Pyjama Party! You and Nilesh Kane. Nilesh Kane. Most politicians are unglamorous, but

Nilesh Kane? No amount of make-up and lighting would make him a less ugly man. Maybe surgery! No, not even surgery! Oh, and remember his hunger strike? I'm told he's killed people. Killed people! Although I imagine if you had to stare at him for a very long time you would most definitely want to kill yourself.

'Do you know he once called me up and asked me to launch his nephew in films? "Make him a star," he said. The boy was seven years old! Just seven years old! He was completely spoilt. At seven years he was already fatter than his uncle. His face was the size of a huge paratha. I took one look at him and told his uncle to get him on a food show. That would be right for the boy. Yup, I told Nilesh Kane to get his nephew on a food show, what I didn't tell him was to get him on as the food.'

Nilesh Kane called Karl Marshall over to his house to draw up the battle plans. Nilesh was on a treadmill, though one couldn't be certain he was actually moving. The treadmill had a unique feature. It had a chair attached to its end, allowing the occupant to take a breather every now and then. Nilesh told Karl of his love of exercise. He said that in his youth he had been a wrestler. For a moment, Karl imagined Nilesh Kane in spandex. He fought the urge to throw up.

Nilesh: I find exercise is very comforting. You'll realize thee healthy mind is because of thee healthy body.

As he spoke, his large stomach and chest jiggled and seemed to take on a life of their own. Karl worried for Nilesh's safety; it looked as if any moment now, his stomach would take off and smash into his face. And the more Nilesh Kane lunged forward, the more likely it was that his third chin would merge into his stomach, forming one large, uncultivated land mass.

'You will be standing from your home constituency, south Mumbai. We have outlined thee plan of action, which I call POA. For thee next 30 days, your itinerary is fixed. It is very tight. Even thee toilet break cannot be increased. That is why we tell all senior politicians to wear diapers. For thee next 30 days, you are at thee war. Kasturikangan will take you through it. He's in charge of your campaign. I myself am going to be very busy as I am standing from five constituencies. Not because I'm worried about winning but because ours is a new party and people are voting because of me, so I need to be everywhere. Kasturikangan, meet Karl Marshall, and please don't ask for thee autograph eh, haha…'

Laughing harder than was safe, Nilesh Kane bent too far forward, Newton's law of gravity took over, and the land mass toppled off the treadmill. As hundreds of supporters rushed forward to help stop a heart attack and offer their support to Nilesh Kane, Karl turned to Kasturikangan.

Kasturikangan was a strange man who was bent parallel at the hip. Consequently, he was often mistaken for an ironing board. He always wore a green safari suit and had a shock of white hair and a pair of horn-rimmed glasses. But the problem with Kasturikangan was the volume of his speech—he couldn't ever really be heard.

For a good five minutes, Karl stared at the old man. Not getting any response, Karl reached out and touched him on his back. Kasturikangan squealed and bolted. For a second, his frame stood upright. Then he folded up again and vaguely, very faintly, Karl began to detect some sound. Karl assumed an ironing board position himself in order to facilitate better communication.

Karl: Hi, I'm Karl. Mr Kane said you're going to be in charge of my itinerary, Mr Kasturikangan?

Mr Kasturikangan tilted his head upwards, marginally above the level of his fallen torso.

Mr Kasturikangan: See, it is like this. We have to look at your weak points and strong points. First, your strong points. [Kasturikangan paused, then swallowed some air and went on.] Okay, now then, let's look at your weak points. You are too young, you are an elitist. You are not from farming or labour class society. You have not been to jail. You do not have any physical handicap like blindness or deafness, which we can exploit. You don't have any terminal disease, at least not yet. You always wear Western attire. Your shoulders are too broad, your waist is too thin. You don't chew paan or tambakoo. You don't have 25 impending court cases on hand, you have no chamchas, you self-drive your car... it is actually quite hopeless. How can I position you as a successful politician if you don't have the necessary qualities? [By now, Kasturikangan's torso being absolutely parallel to the ground, he was almost impossible to hear, and to gain a vantage point, Karl slipped under him.]

Karl: There is one thing.

Kasturikangan: What?

Karl: Haemorrhoids. I'm suffering from piles. When it comes, it's excruciatingly painful, almost like... [He was about to say 'your back' when better sense prevailed.]

Kasturikangan: Excellent, now you are thinking straight. But politics is a very competitive place. We need to fabricate a little to enhance the suffering. The haemorrhoids have spread like a cancer, your legs, arms, vital organs, head are all affected by the dreaded haemorrhoids—that secular killer that doesn't differentiate between Hindu, Muslim, upper caste, lower caste, rich, poor, boy, or girl. Do you see the parallel here? Aah, good. The haemorrhoids have finally manifested into a lung disease, which is causing breathing to become almost impossible. Yet each painful breath is taken because the people need you. Each second of suffering is brushed aside for your desire to propagate all that is good for society. Each breath is laboured, but this does not hinder your vision of leaving a greener, more peaceful and prosperous India behind you after your death. Here was a Caesar—when comes such another?

At the end of the proclamation, Kasturikangan began to weep.

Kasturikangan: By the way...er, what...er, exactly is haemorrhoiditis?

Karl: No, no. It's 'haemorrhoids'—it's a swollen area around the anus. Actually, it cannot...er, medically spread to your arms, legs, and brain. So far, in the history of the disease, no one really has ever been recorded to have haemorrhoids of the...elbow or shoulder...or...

Kasturikangan: Did you say anus?

Karl: Yes. Anus. [Karl said it again and again as he could tell it was making the ironing board uncomfortable.] Anus, anus, A-N-U-S.

Kasturikangan (almost standing erect with shock): No one should know your disease is linked to your... er...er...

Karl: ANUS!

Kasturikangan: Yes, you cannot mention that word. People will stop sympathizing. Politicians must always have terminal diseases from clean areas like brain, lungs, kidneys, shoulders...in some special cases heart is also acceptable. So we will have to review this...er, haemorrhoids. What else have you got?

Karl: Er...acne!

Kasturikangan: Now that is a clean disease. Completely acceptable. The acne is spreading over your body like a tornado. Your arms, legs, chest, brain, are all enveloped by this tenacious disease. Doctors say it is only a matter of time, yet you soldier on because of your love of the people. Your desire to serve the nation selflessly is greater than your boundless pain.

Karl: But I'm not in pain.

Kasturikangan: The moment you enter politics, everybody is in pain, and I don't mean just the general public.

Karl: But people have medical knowledge today. They'll know we are lying.

Kasturikangan: You are an award-winning actor;

you act! People believe what they see. So go ahead, show me painful acne.

Karl made a face like a goldfish flung in the air.

Kasturikangan: Excellent. The pain racking your body is pushed to the back of your powerful mind. You know that you are here to respond to a higher calling. The people need you, the country needs you, the world needs you, so fight on Karl Marshall. Karl Marshall ki jai, Pyjama Party ki jai, Nilesh Kane ki jai!'

Next, Karl was introduced to the contemporary politician's strongest weapon. This was neither commitment, popularity, motivation, drive, cash nor social status; it was the teleprompter. Karl loved the gadget. Initially, Kasturikangan made him practise with it at the office. The only problem was, if it stopped working, then what? Seasoned campaigner that he was, Kasturikangan brushed off this triviality.

Kasturikangan: In such a scenario, all you have to do is repeat your last line again and again until you are overcome with emotion, at which the crowd, most of whom have been paid anyway, will drown you out with applause. For example, if your last line when the machine stops is 'integrity of the nation' or 'food, water, and electricity' or 'jobs for everyone', you just have to keep repeating the phrase as if you are in a trance.

Karl: Yes, but what if the line is some thing else like, 'Excuse me, I need to use the toilet'?

Kasturikangan: No problem, just try it. 'Excuse me, I need to use the toilet, I need to use the toilet, I need to use the toilet, I need to...' [Here, Kasturikangan mimicked massive applause].

Karl looked at him blankly. Was there a chance that Kasturikangan was raving mad? Was it possible that he was being advised and guided by an absolute lunatic? Watching Kasturikangan repeat the toilet line, and simultaneously clap (which he did with two hands awkwardly placed above his bent torso and head), Karl was convinced that in a fair world, in a just society, Kasturikangan would never have been allowed to stray outside the circus.

The campaign trail ran through all sorts of pickets and pockets in south Mumbai. The speeches would be in Hindi, Marathi, and even English, depending on the location. Kasturikangan made sure the speeches weren't very long; Karl, however, realized the people were more interested in seeing Karl the star. They preferred that he did a dance or a dialogue from one of the Munshi Brothers hits. Soon, the teleprompter and speeches were consigned to the dustbin, and all Karl did was a little jig, a couple of lines from his last release, and then have the DJ play his last hit song, which he would lip-sync along with the audience.

Kasturikangan took all this very badly. He was infuriated that his speeches were going to waste. Unable to bear this travesty of political form and decorum, on one occasion he went up on stage and began to recite Karl's prepared speech. Unable to hear him clearly, and seeing a man bent parallel at the hip, the crowd thought it was part of some comedy act and egged him on, laughing at his every line, infuriating the old man further. His passionate discourse on Karl's suffering from acne and his love and loyalty for the country was greeted by derisive

213

hoots of laughter. Hurt and angry, Kasturikangan's voice became more agitated and shrill. As he ranted and raved incomprehensibly, the crowd became restless and began chanting for Karl. When Karl appeared on stage, a huge cheer went up. Kasturikangan, thinking it was for him, raised his head in acknowledgement, placing it almost in line with his stomach. It was the last time he raised his head. In the meantime, the crowd had taken over. Wanting a suitable end to this comic caper, they screamed en masse for Karl to sit on Kasturikangan's unique torso. Ever the showman, Karl obliged. The frail Kasturikangan collapsed into pieces. The crowd screamed their appreciation, and soon afterward, every newspaper and channel flashed the picture of the Pyjama Party's brand ambassador sitting on a 77-year-old human ironing board. With this single act, the Pyjama Party's profile leapfrogged over its competition. The next day, the media ratings showed Karl as the leading candidate in the fray.

Karl tried telling Kasturikangan to look at the bright side and be glad that Karl had sat on him, and not Nilesh Kane. But Karl's quips fell on deaf ears. During the moment of impact, many old, and long-dormant organs finally gave way. The humiliation and shame finished him off. Kasturikangan had become obsolete; he was never heard of again. Truth be told though, whenever Karl visited furniture shops in the future, he could not help but be reminded of the man who had been known by names such as 'The Human Ironing Board', 'The Flaccid One', 'The Bent Bougainvillea', etc.

chapter 10

A few days later, on one of their increasingly rare evenings together, Karl and Kunal had the following conversation.

Kunal: You know, if you are going to canvass for votes, you must do a padyatra.

Karl: What's that? A hotel?

Kunal: No, no…it's a padyatra, you know, a walkabout in your constituency to connect with the aam aadmi, the common man.

Karl: Will there be touching involved?

Kunal: Briefly.

Karl: But what sort of leader walks around the park when he can be driven around in his Mercedes?

Kunal: That's a tough one. The way I see it, you have two choices. Two images. One, you enter like a star with fancy cars and plenty of glamour, and second, you dress down and pretend to be one of them.

Karl: Who's them?

Kunal: You know, those people.

Karl: But who are those people?

Kunal: Arrey baba…that 'type' of people.

Karl: But who exactly are the 'type' of people? Who's them? Who's those?

Kunal: You know, DM types?

Karl: DM types?

Kunal: Yes, yes. Do I have to spell it out to you? Downmarket types, you know. Men who wear vests inside their shirts, women who never change out of their sarees.

Karl: I think I'll stick with the Mercedes.

Kunal: It'll never work.

Kunal, however, had sowed the seed of curiosity. In a few days, Karl agreed on a DMPY or as history has called it since, a downmarket padyatra. After consulting with Nilesh Kane and friends, Karl found to his relief that no one really did much actual walking. Everything would be stage managed, even better than in the movies. As Kane keenly observed, 'All thee politicians are not as feeet as me, most are so fat they can hardly walk. That's why hundred years ago some smart politician eenvented the kurta.'

So here's how the DMPY played out. First they landed in Lalbaugh in Parel, and the car stopped twenty feet away from the houses they intended to visit. Then led by Karl and Nilesh Kane, the Pyjama Party descended on the colony in full force. Water was splashed on Karl's face to make it look as if he was sweating profusely after the long walk. Nilesh Kane who was already sweating buckets also insisted on the same treatment, and hence looked like a man who had just jumped into a swimming pool fully clothed. Nilesh then picked up a two-year-old boy as had been pre-planned and put him on his shoulder. Thankfully, he was already wet, or else he may have felt and noticed the blotch of urine that stayed on his shoulder well after the child had been taken back by the well-paid mercenaries...who also doubled as his parents, for a price of course. Nilesh was dismayed that the crowd seemed more interested in Karl than in himself, and in a desperate bid for attention he began to hug the junta incessantly, downmarket or otherwise. Sarees were given out along with boxes of mithai. The crowd reacted in a typically Indian manner, with people beating each other up in a mad rush to get their hands on the freebies. This was the signal for Kane and company to exit surreptitiously. Quite predictably, Kane pushed and mauled everyone who got in his way, including his own bodyguards, as by now Nilesh Kane's sweaty, protoplasmic form needed the car's air-conditioning as quickly as possible.

Each street brought new experiences. In Byculla, two cheeky teenagers pinched Nilesh Kane's bottom as he gave out free blankets. Since Kane didn't seem to react, Karl figured it had to be for one of two reasons. One, he enjoyed it. Or two, there was way too much blubber to allow for any feeling or response to stimuli.

On Marine Drive, Nilesh Kane outdid himself. He promised to increase the promenade space by reclaiming hundreds of metres from the sea. When an educated scientist type shouted that this was not scientifically possible, he showed his skill as a politician by singing loudly to drown out the dissenting voice. This sort of backfired, as two verses of 'We Shall Overcome' from Nilesh Kane in his native tongue seemed to convince the voters to vote for the dissenting scientific voice instead, who though clearly a pessimist and prophet of doom had the good sense not to sing.

Most of the fun was reserved for Malabar Hill. Now, one must emphasize that Malabar Hill is one of Mumbai's most affluent and educated areas, whose residents don't think highly of politicians in general. Karl was joined by Kunal and both were given a warm welcome. But when Nilesh Kane began to gabble and sweat, people clapped and cheered wildly. Misunderstanding this to be a genuine thumbs-up, Nilesh decided to get into the filmi spirit and do what he thought was a Bollywood dance, but what the audience was convinced was a hippopotamus shaking off water after a bath. It was only when people started returning the blankets that Nilesh Kane stopped and beat a hasty retreat.

In the meantime, Karl was growing in popularity. He used a simple and effective method. Let Nilesh Kane strut his stuff first, and whatever followed second would always be appreciated. Kane for his part thought that the padyatra was his 'greatest triumph ever'.

Nilesh Kane: Deed you see thee way they came to me? That ees love. They wanted to smell me, keese me, hug me, love me. That ees love.

Karl couldn't help but think of those two boys from Byculla who had attempted to beard the lion in his own den, so to speak. But there was a lesson to be learnt. In order to succeed in politics, every moment had to be rehearsed and then executed like a piece of theatre. How ironical. Quite obviously, he was almost certainly the right man for the job.

The DMPY ended on a peculiar note. The final

stretch led to the grand Gateway of India on Mumbai's southern tip. As dusk approached, several dogs went about their evening walks. Dogs, as you probably know, are generally predisposed to be apolitical. Karl and Kunal patted a particularly majestic-looking German Shepherd. Nilesh Kane, trying to show that he too was at one with nature, followed suit. Until then, neither Karl nor Kunal had seen Nilesh Kane sprint. But sprint he did as the German Shepherd decided it was time for an appetizer and ordered some Kane on toast. It wasn't a bad bite, being more of a nip, but it was enough for Kane to run screaming up the stretch before the Gateway. Applause followed, though one couldn't quite tell whether it was for the dog or for Kane's sprint.

Later, Kane yelled violently at his followers.

Nilesh Kane: Whose idea it was to pet thee dog? Huh?

No one responded, as it was pointless reminding Kane that it was he himself who had suggested the move.

Nilesh Kane: It must have been set up by thee Congress. It must have been a Congress dog.

Karl: No sir, it wasn't Congress.

Nilesh: Then eet must have been BJP.

Karl: No sir, not BJP.

Nilesh: Eet must have been something!

Karl: Yes, the dog was Communist.

Nilesh: See. I told you. I knew eet. Otherwise dogs love me. Eet had to be a Communist doggy. Er…how did you know the dog was Communist?

Karl: Because his name was Marx.

For once, Nilesh Kane saw the funny side of it, and laughed aloud. Karl for his part was getting more and more accustomed to the oddities of politics.

What followed next was—as they say—history. No, make that, politics…well, no, actually political history. All right, to be precise, what followed was a historic moment in the political history of the small island of Bombay, now known as Mumbai. Karl Marshall swept his constituency, leaving heavyweights from the Congress, BJP, and other regional parties far behind. It wasn't just a victory, it was a landslide. In cricketing terms, it was an innings and 226 runs victory; in football terms, it was a whopping sixteen goals to zero; in synchronized swimming terms, it was…okay, let's just stick to cricket and football. Nilesh Kane won in four constituencies, thus setting a world record. Not because he won from four different locations but because *he* won from four different locations in spite of being Nilesh Kane.

The Pyjama Party rode on the perfect mix: the rustic charm and ordinariness of Nilesh Kane, the charisma of leading film stars, and a new party and symbol. The message that was sent out was both humorous and positive.

Three immediate effects of the Pyjama Party's performance became evident. The sale of pyjamas skyrocketed. The popularity of the Munshi Brothers' franchise grew even further. And people stopped to add bold brushstrokes of nose hair to posters of Nilesh Kane plastered all over the city. If the victory was ridiculous, the party for the Party was infinitely worse.

Nilesh Kane held centre stage at a huge entertainment room in a five-star hotel. After consuming sixteen flasks and two breweries of alcohol, Nilesh decided to do his version of the pole dance, except that instead of a pole he used his ramrod straight secretary, Madhur Dikshit. Dikshit, whose surname was a hit among Americans (they loved to introduce him to others as the Indian guy who called himself Dik-Shit, followed by machine gun laughter), participated helplessly. The striptease that followed meant that in no time Nilesh Kane's kurta, pyjama, waistcoat, and sandals were draped over Dikshit's arms and shoulders. The underwear wrapped around Dikshit's head brought the house down with mirth. When Nilesh Kane motioned for Karl to follow suit, Karl offered to resign from his constituency. When Nilesh personally offered to help Karl remove his clothes, Karl did the only thing he could do when pushed to the brink—he feigned a heart attack.

As the congratulations continued to pour in the next evening, Karl was summoned to Nilesh Kane's durbar. Both men were sufficiently hung over. But Karl wasn't prepared for the sight that greeted him, drink or no drink. A beached whale lay spreadeagled on a huge sofa. Three nubile young girls were massaging the whale. The whale was separated from society by just the thinnest of towels.

The whale pushed its head out from under the towel, and fold after fold of skin undulated slowly, allowing Nilesh Kane's damaged voice to become faintly audible. As he was being massaged, Nilesh sighed, 'Ah, Karloo, you have come. Can you stand behind me please? My eyes hurt my head if I try to focus.'

He then blinked like a drunk staring at a bright light.

Karl: Congratulations, sir, on your victory, but I just want to ask you one very important question.

Nilesh: Go ahead, but don't shout. My ears are blocked and in thee nose my bridge is running loose.

Karl: Sir, now that I've won the south Mumbai seat, what do I...er, do?

Nilesh (laughing): You do what everybody who wins for the first time does.

Karl: What is that?

Nilesh: Nothing. Absolutely nothing.

Karl: You mean as a Member of Parliament I do nothing, no activity, no work, no constructive contribution, nothing?

Nilesh: Nothing, absolutely nothing...

The rest of what Nilesh said was lost in a groan, as a girl's bracelet got caught in one of his numerous chin folds. As the other two girls rescued their friend's forearm and bracelet, Nilesh Kane continued.

'For thee first three or four times that a politician is elected, he does nothing. Thee weaker ones, ones who are genetically predisposed to stumble on to thee fifth or sixth re-elections, may start to develop a conscience. That ees why many a promising political career ees neepped in thee buds when thee politician is still just in his meed-seventies. Don't worry, now ees thee time to do nothing. It is thee only way to ensure thee country's happiness and welfare. Owww...'

At this point, Nilesh Kane bit his own lip and it

took all three beauties to calm him down. Deciding to let beached whales with thin towels stay beached, Karl thought it prudent to leave. And that was exactly what he did.

The next day, Karl was to be sworn in as Member of Parliament. He decided to go for a walk with Sophia and Kunal to clear his mind. He needed to put everything in perspective, think clearly, hit upon a mature vision, and steer the ship righteously. In order to brace themselves for the future, all three drank very heavily.

epilogue

Within seconds of completing this story, I've been besieged by e-mails from interested readers asking what happened to the other characters. Where did Kunal go from here? Did Karl quit Bollywood forever? What happened to Yusuf Khan? Answering all these questions will take some time...well, at least 45 seconds. Let's turn the clock forward a couple of years and see what fate had in store for our motley crew.

Yusuf Khan, the triumphant thespian, climbed the mountains, and scaled their peaks. Having reached the zenith of his career as an entertainer, Yusuf started looking for more fulfilling experiences, and found peace in the fascinating sport of mountaineering. Having scaled Kanchenjunga and K2, he set his sights on Mount Everest. Quite evidently, the old competitive spirit hadn't died out, and soon he became obsessed with the idea of creating and breaking mountaineering records. He began training to scale Kanchenjunga using only one foot—a feat that had been achieved only once before by a mountaineer called Christian Kuhn. Of course, poor Kuhn had been born with just one foot and didn't really have a choice in the matter. Mountains and climbing became Yusuf's life, and since cellphones don't work above a certain altitude, his contact with the outside world became minimal. That was something nobody complained about, though.

While Yusuf climbed mountains, Karl was drawn into the cesspool of politics, and perhaps the deeper cesspool of marriage. Kunal launched his solo acting career. Within a year, he had carved a niche for himself as the country's biggest (pun intended) action hero. In fact, he was credited with having single-handedly revived the genre. He did this by following a simple maxim—'never do your own stunts'. His biggest success was as a superhero character originally developed for Yusuf Khan, called 'Duckman'. Bitten by a radioactive duck during a routine examination at a highly sensitive government agency research lab, researcher Kumar Saxena was transformed into Duckman, with superpowers to boot. Consequently, he could now do all the things a duck does. *Duckman* had a profound impact on the Indian psyche, starved as it was for a God-like persona who would unite the country, and destroy evil forces, while carrying off bright purple skin-tight suits with elan. *Duckman* fitted the bill, if you'll excuse the pun. On the personal front, Kunal dated a slew of models and Bollywood actresses and so rapidly did he change lovers that unkind cities referred to him as 'Duckman' on screen and 'Rabbitman' off screen. On the business front, Kunal and Karl started a chain of restaurants called Munshi Ka Dhaba, which became so popular that they had to begin a membership scheme to stem the unmanageable crowds. Kunal's parents, unable to withstand the overwhelming response to the *Duckman* series, retired to a serene bungalow in Panchgani, gifted to them by their superstar son. Here they could pursue their lifelong passions of knitting and coughing in peace.

Jehaan finally found the courage to join a choir, called The Have-Nots, and although Jehaan's voice had shifted from tenor to baritone, he had a spring in his step, and a new-found confidence. Of course, the flip side was that at social gatherings or parties, he was like a time bomb waiting to go off. He could break into a song at any moment—something the others at the gatherings lived in perpetual fear of. Maria joined an NGO that focused on elderly people who had been abandoned by their families. Maria's tender and soothingly maternal manner meant that most of the 'oldies' soon began to prefer being abandoned by their families. Of course, the oldies also joked rather unkindly that Jehaan and Maria were the 'Seen and Heard Couple'—Maria shouldn't be seen and Jehaan shouldn't be heard.

Sophia started a photography school where people from all walks of life could come and learn photography for free. Photography, an expensive profession, was beyond the reach of many an aspiring young lensman, so the school did roaring business. The only problem was that the lenses and cameras got nuked routinely, and never before in the history of business did a successful business routinely lose so much money. Like most people who prefer canines to children, Sophia never regretted her decision not to have children. Dogs prove to be more loving and far less high-maintenance, and you don't have to worry about getting them into privileged schools.

The Pyjama Party's success allowed Nilesh Kane to become the undisputed kingmaker, providing critical support to one of the bigger parties. As he began to wield more and more political clout, Nilesh was increasingly influenced by Karl. His dress sense became atrocious—his tight muscle tees and ill-fitting jeans were an awfully embarrassing sight. The jeans were worn well below the Nilesh belly, which had grown with his political prominence, and the muscle tee made him look like a bunched-up mattress. His long-cherished dream of starring in a Bollywood film was realized when Kunal allowed his shadow to appear in the background in all the *Duckman* films. Nilesh Kane was delighted that he had raised the bar and set standards both in glamour and politics. Having begun to consult a stylist, one of Nilesh Kane's moments of greatest glory was when he walked into a party meeting with dreadlocks and tights. He mistook the applause and laughter all around him as signs of the deepest appreciation.

And what of Karl? Well, he tried. For the first six months, he actually looked into housing disputes, water shortages, electricity frauds, the paving of roads, and even cases of domestic abuse. But not a single issue could be resolved positively. Most files remained buried in red tape and paperwork, which Karl soon realized was designed precisely to maintain the status quo. Nothing changed. For instance, if Karl promised an electricity connection to an area, the MSEB or the BMC, or the builder conspired to ensure that he ultimately failed to deliver on his promise. Initially, Karl chastised and threatened the errant parties. But soon Indian politics' best-kept secret dawned on him—that a Member of Parliament has the least power of all. Routinely, he would go to Delhi, attend Parliament sessions, pout, and sign autographs. Eventually, he'd go to Delhi only to sign autographs.

One day, Kunal rushed in.

Kunal: I'm bored.

Karl: You're bored! You're bored? I'm so bored right now that I'd find a glass of water interesting.

Kunal: I can't do these movies any more. For one thing, I can't fit into my Duckman costumes any more.

Karl: Maybe you would if you ate less than twelve times a day.

Kunal: No, it's not me. Spandex actually gets tighter and tighter with use. Sometimes when I'm running in my suit, I can actually feel it getting tighter…like a boa constrictor.

Karl: I'm still bored.

Kunal: Let's do something different. Forget politics, forget the movies, let's run away with these two nice Russian girls I met on the set.

Karl: What about Sophia?

Kunal: She can come too.

Karl: I don't think she's that bored.

Kunal: Okay, we'll put the holiday on hold. Let's start with some of our old tricks instead.

Karl: Can you still do the three-fingers-in-the nose trick I taught you?

Just then, they were rudely interrupted by a member of the Pyjama Party who hurried Karl into a corner and unleashed a bout of urgent whispers. When he had finished, Karl turned to Kunal and said, 'Nilesh Kane has gone bananas.'

Kunal: You mean he's on an exclusive diet.

Karl: No, you idiot. He's just lost it. He's left his wife after knocking up a Russian girl called Nikita on your film set, *Duckman: The Duck Marches On*.

Kunal: What are you saying? Oh God, not Nikita! That's worse than *Beauty and the Beast*. It's like mating a Komodo dragon with a blue jay.

Karl: Wait, there's more. He's left the party for now, so the guys want me to take over.

Kunal: Frankly, if I were you, I'd rather fill in for Nilesh with the Russian girl.

Karl: The president of the Pyjama Party, the mover and shaker, the one-man supreme command of the party, is gone. Do you know what this means?

Kunal: I can no longer perform my nose trick?

Karl: It means that with the general elections set for next year, I could well be an extremely dark, darker than dark, horse for the Prime Minister's post if we manage to form the right alliance and all goes well.

Kunal: See, I have all fingers in one nostril without twitching a single facial muscle. Check it out. Can *you* still do that, Mr Prime Minister?

Karl: Kunal, it's time to get on board. I'm back, we're back. This is the moment I've been waiting for! Now I can actually begin to make a change.

'Let it be known that I unhesitatingly accept the leadership of the Pyjama Party,' Karl said turning to his party colleague.

But by then, Kunal had entered his coughing spasm,

which usually allowed him to resurface for breath only every seventeen coughs. Duckman clearly wasn't listening as the country's future Prime Minister waxed on eloquent.

'I think I've learnt my lesson. It's only as PM that I will be taken seriously. Then and only then will I be able to make a difference. Everything I've done before—school, college, radio, theatre, film—means nothing. I was meant for this and this alone.'

As his voice began to project itself theatrically to an imaginary audience, Karl was interrupted by his wife: 'Mr Prime Minister, can you keep your voice down, as you go about changing India? The dogs can't sleep because of the noise.'

Karl knew better than to argue with a lady. For the moment, he decided to let sleeping dogs lie.

acknowledgements

My watchman Vijay, Oval Maidan, Kunal Vijayakar, Giselle, my 40 pound dumbbells, MTV, CNN-IBN, pornographers the world over, the Sistine Chapel, Friday, and last but hardly least St Xaviers College, The Greatest Educational Institute in the World where I spent the best five years of my life. Also, Radio Mirchi, Rosie, Nirmala and Brian Lara—I thank you all, though without any financial token.

about the author

The author was born many years ago, give and take a day. Over several decades he has refused to grow up.

A few facts about the author:
- He was born left-handed, yet flosses and brushes with his right hand.
- Has been a woman for seven years, but has lately changed his mind. (This is clearly a consequence of having been a lady for far too long.)
- Has tremendous influence and power within the higher echelons of Random House.
- Has written the first four pages, as well as two paragraphs on page 37, all by himself.

Awards:
The author has won many awards, including the second prize in the potato race for class 2G in 1980; The Royal Palm, The Blue Diamond, and The Purple Rose of Cairo awards—all for casual conversation.

Inspirations:
Include Chekhov (not Anton but Dimitri), Cervantes (not Miguel but Manuel), and Bronte (not Emily but both her parents and their English mastiff, Spot).

Author's note:
Much against my will, and under severe duress, I have been coerced into writing this book. If I am found dead by the end of it, please arrest the publisher forthwith.